Dedication

This book is dedicated to the two most important people in my life. Thank you, Alex and Larry, for your unwavering encouragement and support of my writing adventure, your remarkable patience with my incessant questions, and most of all, for making me laugh every day. You make every day a gift, an opportunity, a mystery, an adventure, and a challenge.

Death by Coconut

The Holly Swimsuit Mystery Series, Volume 7

Susie Black

Published by Susie Black, 2026.

DEATH BY COCONUT

First edition. April 11, 2026.

ISBN: 979-8995626114

Written by Susie Black.

Table of Contents

This book is dedicated to the two most important people in my life. Thank you, Alex and Larry, for your unwavering encouragement and support of my writing adventure, your remarkable patience with my incessant questions, and most of all, for making me laugh every day. You make every day a gift, an opportunity, a mystery, an adventure, and a challenge.

Man plans and God laughs...

Acknowledgements:

Thank you, Debbie Walton, for introducing me to the wacky world of cozy mysteries.

Thank you, Terry Newman, Nancy Brashear, Cyndi Stewart, Barbara Newhart, Kimberly Baer, Corinne La Balme, Michelle Godard-Richer, Mark Edward Jones, Brett Wallich, Brian Anderson, Carl Lee, Anastasia Abboud, Avis Adams, Deborah Apodaca, and Nancy Light for your advice, unwavering support, guidance, and most importantly, for always telling me what you think instead of what you think I want to hear... no matter what...

Credits:

Book Cover: Tambi Smith
Editor: Dianne Rich

Praise for Death by Coconut

"This is a funny and thoroughly enjoyable cozy mystery!" ~ **Dianne Harman, USA Today Bestselling Author**

"She may be short of stature, but Holly Schlivnik has attitude to spare."~ **Ellen Byerrum, author of the Crime of Fashion series**

"The well-drawn suspects kept me guessing throughout the story." ~ **Nancy J. Cohen, author of the Bad Hair Day Mysteries**

"Who knew the swimsuit business was so full of intrigue?"~ **Charlotte Rains Dixon, author of Emma Jean's Bad Behavior**

Chapter One

A wave of hot, sticky air enveloped us like a damp blanket as the Art Deco lobby's automatic front doors of the historic Caribe Royale Hotel whooshed open, and the Yentas and I stepped outside.

The butterscotch sun had just risen into the mother-of-pearl bluish-gray sky, and the temperature had already hit a toasty eighty-nine degrees. The humidity rode in on the frothy waves of the aquamarine Atlantic and crawled ashore. It slung low on the hips of the city, clinging to them as snugly as a pair of sodden jeans would to your tush.

The muggy air was so thick you could chew it. It was impossible to go outside and stay dry, let alone clean, on such a sweltering mid-July morning. The Yentas and I already looked as if we'd slept in our wrinkled clothes. Only my mother, used to the steamy weather, was fresh as a daisy on the first day of the annual Miami Swimwear trade show.

The Yentas: Joan Binder, Hope Greenberg, Queenie Levine, Sonia Wilson, and I have met each workday morning for coffee in the California Apparel Mart for over two years. Now, my colleagues and I took our act on the road. By the way, I am Holly Schlivnik, President of Mermaid Swimwear.

Joan wiped a sheen of perspiration dotting her forehead with a swipe of her wrist. She motioned to the line of taxis stationed in front of the hotel and whined like a cranky toddler. "For crying out loud, ladies. I've only taken two steps out of the hotel, and I'm already drowning in my sweat. Why are we walking and not taking an air-conditioned cab?"

I pointed to the Brews & Bagels coffee shop, located on the ground floor of the building next door to the hotel. "Because, Joanie, the coffee shop is about five hundred feet from the spot you're standing on. The cab meter charges by the mile, not by the foot."

Joan glared with her well-practiced kindergarten teacher's look of disapproval and tossed out one of her famous snarky zingers. "Did the geniuses at the swim association choose this outdoor steam bath as the next best locale to hold the trade show at because the Amazon jungle was already booked?"

Hope tipped her head to the side like my dog Siggie does when he's trying to understand something. "Joan, what are you talking about? The show is held inside the convention center, not outdoors."

As we walked to the coffee shop, Sonia, always succinct, answered instead of Joan. "Hope, she was referring to the *city* chosen as the site of the market, not if the market itself is held outdoors..."

I followed the intoxicating aroma of freshly-brewed coffee into the busy cafe five minutes later. My business partner and BFF, Queenie, and I waited in line for coffee and bagels while the others commandeered the only large group table in the back of the restaurant.

We distributed everyone's breakfast, and Queenie smiled at Mom. "Will Mike come down to the show to visit all his schemata buddies?"

Mom shook her head. "No. Mike and one of his retired garment friends are in Monte Carlo at a backgammon tournament."

Joan asked, "Are they contestants or fans?"

Mom said, "Contestants. They belong to a local backgammon club and are excellent players. Mike says they have a good shot of at least placing in the senior tournament."

We no sooner finished eating than Queenie poked me in the ribs with her elbow. She motioned across the store and groaned. "Look at the kook who's coming our way."

I said, "She's a bit flamboyant, but not too bad. We've been on a few industry committees together. She's smart, did her part, and was pleasant. We ate lunch together a few times, and it was enjoyable."

I plastered a way-too-cheery for so early in the morning grin on my kisser as campy competitor Avril Wilts, Vice President of Sales at Tigress Swimwear, sauntered to our table. Decked out in her signature skin-tight tiger print jumpsuit, Avril invited herself to join us by planting her tush into the open seat between my mother and me. She swiveled her head back and forth between my mother and me. "You two look more like sisters than mother and daughter. Holly, I can see how you'll look in twenty years."

I grinned. "Yeah. We get that often."

Avril turned to my mother. "So, Natalie...we're at the beginning of *another new season*. Your boss shops my line every market, but never writes an order. What's a girl gotta do to get a foot in the door at Laurie's?"

Before Mom answered, Joan slammed her hand on the table so hard that the cups flew up and coffee spilled all over.

Joan growled through clenched teeth, "Avril, you're way out of line. Buttonholing is strictly verboten, especially at social gatherings." Joan hitched her thumb to the store exit. "You crashed our coffee klatch uninvited, so if you can't behave professionally, take a hike."

Avril jutted her jaw. "What are you, Joan, the etiquette police?" She glared at my mother. "Pass along a message to Mariel: She will regret it if she doesn't place an order with us this year. I'll go over her head to Mr. Green and complain that since his buyer only gives orders to her industry pets, there's no open-to-buy dollars available for the rest of the vendors."

She pointed an index finger, *j'accuse* style, at each Yenta. "So, Mariel must be on the take...I bet Mr. Green won't be too happy *if that tidbit got out in the market*." She smiled evilly and poked her finger into her ample cleavage. "And I'll make it my business to spread it all over the show."

I burst out laughing. "You couldn't get it more backward if you tried. We do get special treatment, but not the kind you'd want. We receive our orders *dead last*, not first, and fight for our deliveries and open-to-buy dollars the same as all the other suppliers." I pointed to my mother. "Mariel bends over backward not to show favoritism to us because *my mother* works for her."

Avril patted her bouffant hair and rolled her eyes. "I might be a blonde, but I'm not dumb. You're nothing but an entitled liar." Then the sexy ex-model-turned-sales-exec stood, spun on her heels, and stalked out of the coffee shop.

Sonia deadpanned, "There is one woman who missed the lecture on how to make friends and influence people."

Joan pursed her lips. "Sales is certainly not her strong suit. Better to have stayed in modeling. All she had to do was keep her yap shut, twirl around, and smile." Joan pointed to herself. "I'm not exactly the most diplomatic at times, but I've learned the hard way to tone it down because you get more flies with honey than vinegar. How she gets *any orders* is a mystery."

Hope finished mopping the last of the spilled coffee off the table and glanced at my mother. "You're not the buyer; you're the assistant. You have no control over which brands are bought. So, why Avril thought she'd accomplish anything other than pissing you off by harassing you is beyond me."

Queenie curled her upper lip. "The woman is a moron. All her little outburst accomplished was to give herself a feel-good moment." Queenie turned to my mother. "I hope it was worth it to her, because one word from you to Mariel, and Avril will *never* get an order."

Mom shrugged. "Nah. I won't mention Avril's threat and get her in trouble. She's only doing her job."

Joan's eyes popped. "*Why the hell not*? If you don't put a blowhard like Avril in her place, she'll make your life a nightmare."

Mom funneled her lips. "In life, we all get a rope. And you either hang yourself or save yourself with it. I don't have to hang her. If Avril is stupid enough to make good on her threat, she will hang herself."

I held my wrist up and pointed to my watch. "We'd better hustle or we'll be late for our first appointments."

We walked a block and waited at the intersection to cross the street at the light. I stepped one foot off the curb as the signal turned from red to green. Sonia looked up as a strong gust of wind rustled the fronds of a large palm tree next to the traffic light. Sonia shoved me away from the curb and screamed, "Look out, Holly!"

Joan grabbed my arm and pulled me from traffic as a coconut dropped from the top of the palm tree. It whizzed past me so closely that the whoosh of the air ruffled my bangs into my eyes. The coconut hit the ground, and its milk splattered over my shoes as the outer shell shattered into a hundred pieces.

Joan clutched her hands over her heart and gasped. "*Holy guacamole! That was close.*"

Hope slapped her cheeks. "My God, Holly! If not for Sonia's quick reaction, *your head* would be smashed to smithereens."

Sonia held her index finger over her thumb. "You came this close to being killed."

Queenie grinned. "Talk about a novel way to go out...Death by Coconut."

Little did any of us realize how prophetic Queenie's quip would turn out to be.

Chapter Two

We'd just finished showing the line to Martin from Swim N' Surf Stores when Simon Posnick's showroom manager burst into our booth, sobbing. Lucinda Burke staggered across the room, found Lauren Bishop, and threw her arms around our showroom manager's neck. My eyes widened as the normally neat-as-a-pin Lucinda looked as if she'd been run over by a bus.

I'd known identical twins Lauren and Lucinda since I started in the rag business. Yet, if not for a strawberry-shaped beauty mark on Lauren's chin, I still couldn't tell them apart.

Tall, well-proportioned, and shapely with a generous bust, the brunette and green-eyed sisters shared identical looks and had chosen the same career path, but had little else in common. Lauren's personality is outgoing and assertive. Lucinda is shy and reserved. Lauren is happily married and the mother of two rambunctious children. Lucinda barely escaped a terrible marriage and is struggling as a single parent of a special-needs child.

Lauren pried Lucinda's arms from around her neck and led her disheveled sister to the back of the booth. It wasn't my intention to be nosy, but in our inverted cone-shaped booth, it was impossible not to overhear their conversation.

Lauren said, "Luce, get a hold of yourself. I can't understand you when you're crying. Take a breath and *calmly* tell me what's got you so upset."

Lucinda's voice quivered as she hiccupped her reply. "I-it's S-Simon. M-my G-God, h-he's a m-monster!"

Lauren clucked her tongue. "What now?"

Lucinda said, "Jonathan was accepted into the Brighter Day Autism School, and he received a partial scholarship."

Lauren yelped, "That's fantastic news! So, what does that have to do with Simon?"

Lucinda said, "Even including the partial scholarship, the monthly tuition is $2,000.00. At my current salary, I'd face a monthly shortfall of $1,000.00 for all our other bills once tuition is paid. My last raise was two years ago. I asked Simon for a $250.00 weekly raise." Lucinda spat, "He agreed to the raise...if I agreed to *additional duties*."

Lauren asked, "Does he want you to go on the road? He knows you can't leave your son alone."

Lucinda sobbed. "No! He demanded I sleep with him! And threatened to hold back my paycheck if I refused to put out."

Lauren gasped, "Oh come on...he wasn't serious. The man is a gold-medal champion slug, but even he wouldn't dare stoop so low. Is it possible you misunderstood him?"

Lucinda snapped, "He was as serious as a heart attack."

The MeToo Movement somehow missed this jerk.

Lauren shrugged. "You have no choice but to quit. Go back to the booth right now and pack your personal belongings. Give your notice, effective immediately, and then walk out. Leave him in the lurch in the middle of the biggest swimwear market of the year. Hit the jerk in the place where it hurts him the hardest. In his wallet."

Lucinda clucked her tongue. "Quitting is impossible without another job. I already live paycheck to paycheck. I can't be without an income for even a week."

Lauren nodded. "Okay. I get it. Work through the swimwear market and put him off. Say you're considering it. Ask for the particulars. How often? Locations and times? In the meantime, we'll put our feelers out. You're an experienced showroom manager with a good reputation. I'll ask Harriet and Holly for help. Between all of us getting the word out, you'll land somewhere in no time."

Lucinda asked, "And if nothing else is available? Then what? Brighter Day would be a game-changer for Jonathan, but I won't pimp myself out to pay the tuition."

Lauren tsked. "Of course not. Between the folks, Ronnie and me, and the rest of the family, we'll back your play the way we always have."

Lucinda gushed, "You're the best. I..."

The rest of Lucinda's response was obliterated by tall, buff, imposing Simon Posnick storming into our booth.

Thank the Goddess we had no customers.

He turned a one-eighty and yelled at the top of his lungs, "*LUCINDA*! I know you're here. We've got a packed booth of impatient buyers. If one of them leaves because you're not in the booth to show them the line, consider yourself fired!"

I was halfway across the room to throw the jackass out, but he saw me coming and saved me the trouble. He turned about-face and stalked across the hall to his half-empty booth.

Chapter Three

The next day, Avril Wilts and I nodded hello as we met at the ladies' room sinks. I finished washing up first, waved goodbye, and left. I was at the main aisle of the convention center when Avril rushed out and called my name. "Holly, a few minutes, please?"

I sighed. So far, our booth has been packed all day. I'd been on my feet for hours, missed lunch, and this was my first and long-overdue potty break. My back hurt, I was dying to take off my high heels, and I was tired and cranky. The last thing I wanted was Avril Wilts, round two. But my good manners prevailed, and I waited for her.

I said, "If you promise to play nice in the sandbox, I'll walk as far as your booth. Make it short and sweet because we have a full house. I've got to get back to our booth."

She nodded, slipped my arm into the crook of her elbow, and steered us toward the loading dock. "I was hoping I'd run into you. Do you mind taking a slight detour?" She held up a delivery slip. "I need to pick up a box of samples. It won't take more than a minute or two. I promise."

Didn't I say make it short and sweet?

I sighed. "O-kay."

We entered the loading dock delivery office, and Avril handed the clerk her slip. He found her package and had her sign for it. The clerk tapped the top of the package. "This is heavy—weighs thirty-three pounds." The clerk pointed to a line of trolleys next to the metal case. "Wait a sec, and I'll get you a trolley. Make sure you return it before five o'clock when the dock closes."

Avril flexed her biceps. "I can handle a thirty-three-pound carton with no problem."

The clerk shrugged. "Okay, suit yourself, but it's not my fault if you throw your back out."

She picked up the carton, and we headed to the vendor booth aisles.

I asked, "So, what do you want to talk to me about?"

She dipped her head. "I wanted to apologize for yesterday morning."

"You owe me no apology, but my mother is another story," I snarked. "You might consider changing methodologies. Yours stinks."

She puckered her lips. "It doesn't justify my behavior, but I owe you an explanation for my strong-arm tactic yesterday, so you'll understand the context and reason behind it. This season is my sixth at Tigress Swimwear. The owners, Mike and Mickey Larsen, came to me six months ago with a proposition. If I got written commitments from the twelve stores they were the most anxious to sell to by the end of the Miami swimwear show, the Larsens would make me a twenty-five percent minority partner. I've already received written commitments from eight of

the stores. The last four are Florida accounts. I am confident I'll get written commitments from three of the four. Laurie's is the one stickler mucking up the opportunity of a lifetime."

"Why?"

"Because the Larsens will only make good on the partnership if I get written commitments *from all twelve stores*." She held out her hands in supplication. "So, you can see, that's the reason I am so desperate to get a commitment from Mariel."

I sniffed. "You're lucky my mother has a soft spot in her heart for salespeople. If she passed your idiotic threat to Mariel, you'd receive a commitment from Laurie's Stores the second Tuesday of next week."

Avril shrugged. "You can't lose what you don't have. I used the wrong approach, but I still need some help. Now that I've explained my situation, will you ask your mother to help me?"

Good grief. Was English not her first language?

"Since you didn't understand it the first time, I'll speak more slowly so you can comprehend each word. *My mother has no say in which lines Mariel places orders with.*"

Avril rolled her eyes. "Come on, Holly. Cut the crap. Natalie has worked for Mariel for a decade, and you expect me to believe that the woman never asks your mother for her opinion on a line? You don't want to help me...okay. I'm not happy, but don't insult my intelligence by saying your mother doesn't influence her boss."

"Think what you will. But I won't help you or anyone else put my mother in a compromising position with her boss. If you want an order from Mariel Levine, let your product be your best advocate. Mariel is a seasoned, successful buyer who didn't get this far by buying only from her favorite vendors. She buys from vendors whose lines have the styles she *can sell*. If your product is right for her customers, you'll get an order. Here's my advice. Take your designer and merchandiser on a field trip to one of Mariel's stores tonight and see if your product fits into her mix. If yours doesn't, send your design team back to the drawing board."

Avril stopped dead in her tracks two doors down from her booth. She pointed to Simon Posnick and her bosses, deep in conversation. She snarled, "The nerve of the worm. He's still the same sleazeball he was when we worked at the same company. I bet he hid around the corner, waiting for me to leave the booth so he could campaign for my job."

The guy is like a bad penny showing up everywhere.

I grimaced. "You and he worked together? Please accept my condolences."

She nodded. "Yeah, years ago. I was the Sable Swimwear L.A. showroom manager, and Simon was the local rep. We had a brief affair. It went south once I was promoted to Sales Manager over Simon. If I accepted the promotion, he threatened to tell Sam Sable about the affair in the hopes I'd be fired, and he'd get the job."

I looked at her oddly. "So, it didn't occur to him that he'd be fired too?"

She snorted. "Nobody ever said he was the sharpest knife in the drawer. I called his bluff, took the job, and fired him."

Avril laughed mirthlessly. "How he found out is a mystery, but no sooner did the Larsens propose the deal, Simon appeared out of the clear blue and threatened to expose our affair if I didn't pay for his silence."

I rolled my eyes. "Who cares about an ancient history affair?"

She dipped her head to the Tigress booth. "If you went by our sexy product styling, you'd never guess the Larsens are conservative, religious people and would be appalled by the affair between a married man and me."

My eyes popped. "Please tell me you didn't pay the bastard!"

Avril clucked her tongue. "Of course not. I told him to pound sand. Then I heard through the grapevine he had become a multi-line rep, moved to Miami, and out of my hair...or so it seemed." She pointed to Simon, bared her teeth, and growled deep in her throat like a ferocious tiger. "I worked my ass off to get where I am. If the slug tries to take it away from me, I swear to God I'll kill him."

Chapter Four

Saturday morning, I greeted the Yentas and our southeastern sales rep, Harriet Kaplan, who joined us for breakfast.

I glanced at my watch and turned to Harriet. "Is Lauren opening the booth? Someone from our group has to be there when the show starts, or we'll get a hefty fine."

Harriet nodded. "Yes, she is. Lauren lives closer to the convention center than I do, so it's easier for her to get in early than for me. So, we decided that she'll open the booth and I'll close up at the end of each day."

I took a sip of coffee and asked, "Are we all set for tonight's pre-fashion show dinner party?"

Harriet gave me the OK sign. "All taken care of. A six-fifteen reservation for nine of us at Mango Tango. That's the Cuban restaurant that served those fabulous Maduro fried plantains you loved so much last time. The restaurant is within walking distance of the convention center."

Joan counted the guest list. "Holly, Queenie, Hope, Sonia, me, Harriet, Natalie, and Lauren. Eight. Who is the ninth guest?"

I said, "I invited Lucinda to join us."

Hope smiled. "How thoughtful of you."

I said, "She deserves some fun. I'm glad her mom is taking Jonathan for the weekend."

Harriet panned the table and grinned. "Too bad you guys left early last night. You missed all the excitement. Walter Seiden, the Miss Prim Swim rep, showed up at Simon Posnick's booth and accused Simon of stealing Mystique Swimwear from him. Simon ordered Walter out of his booth. Walter refused. Everyone on the aisle heard Simon's threat to have Walter arrested for trespassing. The two got into a fist fight. Nancy Lookofsky from Sweet as Sugar Swimwear called security. Two security guards broke up the fight and escorted the two out of the convention center, kicking and screaming."

Sonia stroked her chin. "It will be interesting to see if they come for the cocktail hour and fashion show."

Hope said, "If they had any self-respect, they'd lie low and hope their customers got no wind of their ruckus."

Joan rolled her eyes. "The only way those two would miss an opportunity to buttonhole buyers is if they got expelled from the trade show. But unless one of them commits a murder, the Swimwear Association won't throw them out and forfeit their revenue."

I clucked my tongue. "We forked out a bucket of bucks for a premium booth location at this market. We should not be subjected to the continued disruptions to our business created by Simon Posnick." I turned to Queenie. "If last night did not get him expelled, you and I had better pay

a visit to Sharon at the Swimwear Association and discuss having Simon kicked out of the show."

Queenie laughed. "We'd be doing him a favor. At the rate he's making enemies, he might not make it through the show in one piece."

Six-forty-five; the evening of the same day.

I checked the time again. Annoyance and worry twisted my heart into knots. I looked across the elegantly set, candle-lit, banquet-style table at Harriet. "This is so unlike the twins not to call if something came up," I snarked. "The question is, do I hug them or slug them if they show up?"

Harriet wrung her hands. "Lauren is extremely responsible. She would never stand anyone up, *least of all her bosses*."

Queenie held out her hands. "You texted her, left voicemail messages, went outside and looked for them. You checked at the reception desk and the restroom. You've already told the maître d' to be on the lookout for the twins. There's nothing more you can do."

I signaled our waiter. "Well, we can't wait any longer for them. If the waiter doesn't put in our orders now, we won't get to eat and still be back at the convention center in time for the fashion show."

An hour and a half later...

Overnight, the convention center theater lobby had been transformed into a jungle. Dozens of palm trees in camouflage planters, interspersed with lush, colorful flowers and plants, and large bamboo cages filled with live tropical birds were placed around the room. The open bar was decorated like a tiki lounge, with six bartenders dressed in brightly colored floral shirts and white trousers, pith helmets adorning their heads.

Queenie pointed to the papier mâché coconuts suspended from the ceiling. "At least if one of those falls on your head, it won't be fatal."

I nudged Harriet. "Any sign of the twins?"

Harriet turned a one-eighty. "Nope. I left Lauren another message, but she didn't respond."

I smacked my knuckles into my palm. "Damn. This is not like them. I hope there's no problem with Jonathan."

I pointed to the packed bar. "Now's the time to belly up to the bar, or we won't get the drinks before the fashion show starts."

I glanced at Queenie and twisted my wrist as though taking a sip. "Your usual scotch on the rocks and a twist?"

She grinned. "You need to ask?"

The others declined, so I powered through the crowd and elbowed my way into a narrow space two rows back from the bar. I caught the attention of one of the bartenders. I funneled my hands around my mouth and shouted my order over the noisy din. He nodded and turned around to assemble the cocktails.

Five minutes later, the bartender brought the drinks back. I tried to move closer to the bar, but it was like I was pushing a car to the side of the road.

I tapped the back of a tall man in front of me and waved the twenty under the guy's nose. Walter Seiden turned around and grinned. "If you're buying, I'm drinking."

I laughed. "I'll take a rain check."

Walter dipped his head. "Okay, so what can I do for you?"

I waved the Jackson like a flag. "Would you let me step in front of you so I can pay the bartender and get my drinks?"

Avril Wilts interrupted Walter's reply by pushing her way between us. "Holly," she waved her arm in an arc around the lobby, "when are your mother and Mariel coming?"

I shrugged. "Contrary to popular opinion, I am not my mother's keeper...But for giggles and squeaks, why do you care?"

I bit my lip not to laugh in Avril's face as Walter indelicately snorted.

Avril said, "Because my bosses are here and I want the five of us to sit together at the fashion show."

I arched a brow. "My dad was considered the swimwear industry's gold medal champion buttonholer, but *you* take it to an art form. Not to burst your bubble, but my mother and Mariel are sitting with my group."

She huffed, " Not if I get to them first." She stomped away, a hunter seeking her prey.

Walter rolled his eyes. "Unreal. The broad has one helluva hard-on for Mariel Levine. Our booths are unfortunately next to one another's, and she constantly bellyaches about the way Mariel shops her line, but always passes."

I said, "Mariel is a professional shopper. It is her job to *shop the entire market*. It's *not her job to buy from every supplier*, only from the ones with the most saleable styles for her customers."

Walter lifted his right wrist and glanced at his watch. "Let's get your drinks handled in time to enjoy them before the fashion show begins." He leaned down and put his hand out. "It's safer for you and easier for me to make the exchange."

I nodded my agreement.

A nasty-looking two-inch gash in the shape of a question mark on his left forearm, scratches on his right, and two sets of bruised knuckles also caught my eye as I handed him the cash. I pointed to the wounds. "That's a gnarly set of scrapes. How'd it happen?"

Walter stared at his arms as though it were the first time he noticed the wounds. "Oh, these?" He held up his arm. "I was in a hurry opening a sample crate and nicked myself on the metal edge."

Nice try, Bucko. Sample case, my Aunt Fanny's tush.

My smile radiated feigned sympathy. "You'd better be examined by a doctor and get some meds before they become infected."

Mr. Macho shrugged.

Walter leaned into the bar and made the exchange. He turned to me and held the drinks up in the air. "Let's get you and your drinks safely away from the mob."

He looked around the room for the least-crowded route. Suddenly, his face turned as purple as a ripe eggplant. His cheek clenched, and a vein throbbed in the middle of his forehead in pure rage. My eyes followed where he was looking. Simon Posnick entered the theater lobby and checked out the crowd.

Oh, joy. Visions of round two—this time, a public fight to the death—flitted across my mind. Before my luck ran out, I pointed to

Queenie and Harriet at the opposite end of the lobby. "Walter, my group is near the back wall."

Walter grunted and pivoted. I followed his lead as he powered through the crowd. We made it to the less-crowded other side of the room.

I smiled. "Thanks so much for the help. I owe you one."

Walter tipped a two-fingered salute, and we parted company.

I spotted Mom and Mariel carrying their cocktails and searching the crowd. Sonia, the tallest of the Yentas, waved and got their attention. The two women muscled through the crowd and joined us in a corner across from the bar.

Mom sipped her standard Chardonnay. Not much of a drinker, she'd nurse it all evening. Mariel held a scooped-out coconut shell with a straw and a cheery miniature umbrella floating inside. Hope and Joan moseyed over to Mariel and eyed the coconut with curiosity. Joan asked, "What's inside the coconut?"

Mariel took a big slurp and smiled. "This is a Batida de Coco. It's a classic Brazilian cocktail similar to a coconut margarita."

Hope asked, "What are the ingredients?"

Joan rolled her eyes. "I'm gonna go out on a limb and say stuff from a coconut."

Mariel nodded. "Yes. It's a mixture of coconut milk, sweetened coconut water, toasted coconut shavings, and Cachaca, a Brazilian rum."

She grinned elfishly. "The first time I tried one was during a January buying trip to Rio. Since Brazil is located south of the equator, it was summer. Their summer weather is the same as ours: hot and humid. So, I should have known better." She held the coconut up to eye level. "But when you add the sweet coconut water, you don't taste the rum, so you don't realize how potent the drink is. And of course, the heat and humidity only added to the potency." She snorted a laugh. "I downed three of these and couldn't stand up on my own for over an hour! I was with a group of other buyers and *my boss*. Talk about embarrassing. Holy moly. It took years to live the episode down. So, now I only allow myself one Batida de Coco and take my time drinking it."

Decked out in a sequin-trimmed tiger print jumpsuit, Avril Wilts spied us from the end of the bar and strode across the room in our direction. Mariel's back stiffened as Avril pushed into our circle and sidled next to Mom's boss.

Avril shoved her wineglass under Mom's nose. "Do me a favor, Natalie, and hold my Merlot a minute so I can do a quick change."

Mom shrugged and took the wineglass.

I muttered, "A quick change into...?"

Queenie whispered, "Making herself disappear."

I batted my eyes. "If only..."

Avril slid a watermelon-shaped tiger print purse off her shoulder. She leaned against a wall and stepped out of tiger print tennis shoes. She unzipped the purse and turned it upside down. It reconfigured itself into two knee-high tiger-print stiletto-heeled boots. She unzipped the boots and separated the tops from the stiletto heels. The remainder was a pair of stiletto pumps. She dropped the tennis shoes inside, zipped the boot tops back up, and shouldered the recreated purse.

I said, "Quite a neat trick, but why perform it now and not before you arrived?"

Avril answered me, but glared at Mariel. "Because our line is *so hot*, we worked nonstop all day." She crossed her legs and grabbed her crotch. " No potty or lunch breaks, or sitting for even a minute. We turned *customers away* so we could get to the fashion theater before the show started."

Queenie fingered the purse and arched a brow. "How veddy James Bond of you..."

Avril grinned. "I prefer to call this my getaway bag."

She took the purse off her shoulder and unzipped it. She held the sides apart, and Queenie and I looked inside. Several zipped compartments of various sizes lined the interior.

Queenie looked deeper inside the purse. "How much can you fit into it?"

Avril pulled the sides of the purse as wide as possible. "This bag is amazing. Over the years, I've packed it with mid-sized sample presentations, a three-day weekend's worth of clothes, shoes, and makeup, and once, even a bowling ball.

She zipped the purse closed and patted its front. "Two quick zips, and presto, I dress an outfit up or down, depending on the occasion, by changing from boots to stilettos."

Avril read Queenie's and Mariel's name tags, looked back and forth between them, and said, "You two have the same last name. Are you related?"

Queenie burst out laughing. "You do realize that all the millions of people with Jones as a last name are not related to one another."

Avril pursed her lips. "If you were related, it would explain how much business you get from Laurie's."

Queenie jutted her chin. "Let's get a couple of things straight right now, Avril. One: You have no idea the size of our business with Laurie's or any of our accounts. Two: The business Mermaid Swimwear gets from *any account, including Laurie's,* is based on one criterion alone—the merit of our product. Favoritism plays no role in the orders we receive."

Avril rolled her eyes. Then she took her wine glass back from my mother, hoisted it, faced Mariel, and made an odd toast. "To future orders. May you write many..." She took a sip of her Merlot and stared steely-eyed at Mariel. "I'm looking forward to our appointment tomorrow. *Bring your order pad. And be prepared to write Tigress an order, for a change.* Pay close attention to the Tigress styles in tonight's fashion show. Those are our hottest items you have to buy." Avril smiled. "Why don't you and Natalie sit with my bosses and me and let us point them out to you so you won't miss them?"

Mariel pursed her lips. "Sorry, but we'll be taking notes for AJ and Bea, our advertising team, and will be too busy selecting items for our billboard style out for any chit-chat."

Avril snapped, "All the more reason to join us."

The parrots and macaws in the cages surrounding our group ruffled their feathers and squawked as Avril punctuated her point, growling like a tiger. She curled her fingers into claws and scraped them across her jumpsuit. Not waiting for Mariel's response, Avril stalked to the other side of the lobby to interrupt her management's conversation with Simon Posnick.

Joan turned to Mariel. "After that stupid stunt, if you keep the appointment, the only thing to do with your order pad is stuff it down Tiger Lily's throat."

Mariel laughed and waved a *Who-gives-a-rat's-ass* gesture with a flip of her wrist.

For once in his life, Simon Posnick used his brain and skedaddled before Avril reached the other side of the room. Unfortunately, he noticed where she came from. Before Mariel could escape, Simon quickly closed the distance between him and our group and cornered her.

In her early fifties, with wavy salt-and-pepper hair, Mariel sported an hourglass figure and stood about five feet four or five. She had mischievous blue eyes, a turned-up nose, and lush lips that were framed by a heart-shaped face.

Mariel's signature radiant smile quickly faded when Simon invaded Mariel's private space by strategically positioning himself between

Mariel, the wall, the bird cages, and my mother, standing next to her boss, so Mariel was trapped.

Harriet leaned over and whispered, "Get a load of Simon. Quite a nasty-looking scratch on his arm and another on the side of his face, and his clothes are disheveled."

I angled my head toward the bar where Walter was still hanging around. "Walter is bruised, too. Maybe Simon and Walter went for round two."

Harriet straightened an imaginary wrinkle on her impeccably neat blouse. "Who comes to an industry event so slovenly?"

I dipped my head. "There are no boundaries or shame to arrogance."

I turned to Simon and touched my cheek. "Simon, your face looks as if you and Walter went a second round."

Simon grazed his fingers across his cheek and sneered. "Your concern is so touching. It's none of your business, but my sister's kitten is the culprit."

Simon dismissed me like a pesky gnat and turned to Mariel. "*Why didn't you return any of my calls?*" He curled his upper lip and snarled. "*I. Need. An. Answer. Now.*"

Mariel clucked her tongue. "I already gave you my answer, and nothing changed. Not a single line in the entire swimwear industry, *least of all your line*, warrants thirty percent of my open-to-buy dollars. And we have neither the space nor the desire to give *any supplier* a store within a store in any, let alone in all, of our locations."

Simon sneered, "You either meet my demands or I'll ruin you in the industry. By the time I get done, you'll be lucky to be a stock clerk at Purdines."

Mariel shrugged. "Knock yourself out. I'll put my industry reputation up against yours any day of the week."

The house lights flashed, indicating that the fashion show would begin in ten minutes. The crowd began making its way to the theater entrance.

Mariel caught my mother's eye. "Come on, Natalie, let's go into the theater. The best seats near the runway will fill quickly, and I want to see all the styles up close."

Simon made a half-turn and blocked their way. "*Where the hell are you going? I'm not finished with you!*"

Mariel rolled her eyes. "But I'm finished with you. Move aside, or you can kiss *any orders* from me goodbye."

Simon lurched forward and grabbed Mariel by the arm. She yanked her arm away but caught part of the sleeve of her silk blouse on the jagged edge of the coconut in her other hand. The fabric swatch ripped off and snagged onto the coconut shell.

Mariel held her arm up and snapped, "Dammit, you big ape. You ruined a hundred-and-fifty-dollar silk shirt. You'll pay for this and more, you jackass." She swept an arm toward the theater entrance. "*Now get out of my way.*"

Simon smirked. "A torn shirt is the least of your problems with me, lady." Simon jutted his jaw. "*We're not finished, Mariel. Not by a long shot.*"

Mariel growled. "Oh, you're dead wrong."

Mariel grabbed my mother's arm and neatly sidestepped around Simon. She stalked to the theater entrance with my mother in tow, and they disappeared inside.

Chapter Five

Seven a.m. Sunday

Joan craned her neck to the coffee shop entrance as Queenie and I served the coffee and bagels to the Yentas. "Aren't we waiting for Harriet and Natalie?"

I shook my head. "No. Harriet went straight to the booth to set up the line and modeling assignments for our Purdines appointment. My mother went to Laurie's executive office for a meeting with Mariel and the store planners to work out floor space for several of the suppliers they are seeing today. Since Mom and Mariel will be working at the market together, they'll come to the convention center in one car. Mom lives closer to the office than she does to the convention center. It'll be easier to go to the office once they're finished shopping, and for her to go home from there."

Sonia widened her eyes. "Considering Mariel's two dustups last night, it's amazing she'd even show up at the convention center today."

Hope surveyed the table. "Could Simon really have something on Mariel so terrible that it would ruin her career if it got out? She has a wonderful reputation in the industry, but I suppose there are skeletons in everyone's closet."

I said, "Mom and I went for coffee after the fashion show. I asked her the same question. She said she questioned Mariel, and the only incident that came to Mariel's mind was that six months into her first job as an assistant buyer at Sayer Brothers in the junior dress department, she was swept up in a payoff scandal involving a dozen buyers, including her boss. The twelve buyers and three assistants were fired, but Mariel and eight other assistants were found not to be complicit. Four of them, including Mariel, were eventually promoted to fill the open buyer positions. But the stigma of the scandal rubbed off on the assistants, and by the end of the year, they all resigned."

Joan screwed up her face. "*That's it?* What a joke." She scoffed. "Girl Scout troops in Beverly Hills are involved in bigger scandals selling cookies."

Sonia stroked her chin. "Mariel's around fiftyish, so it happened *thirty years ago*. Even if she was up to her eyeballs in it, why anyone would give a flying fig about something that happened before half the industry was out of short pants, much less ruin her career, is beyond me."

Queenie snarked, "I bet when Walter Seiden bonked Simon on the head the other night, he scrambled the guy's brains."

Joan bit her lip. "Or, Simon rolled the dice and put out an empty threat to a non-existent incident, hoping a real skeleton lurked in Mariel's closet and she'd panic and give in to his demands."

I said, "The stunt Simon pulled last night is his third strike, and as far as I'm concerned, he should be expelled from participating in the swim show."

Queenie wrinkled her brow. "The market is almost half over. So, why bother if there's no point?"

I said, "The point is, Simon is a menace. If there are no consequences for his actions, he'll be emboldened to do even worse things. I say we go to Sharon and file a formal complaint. If she won't expel him for the rest of this market, at least we can suggest not allowing him to participate in any future ones."

Eight Fifteen a.m. Sunday

As the Yentas and I rounded the corner to our aisle, Queenie and I stopped in our tracks. Simon Posnick's booth was closed. The strictly enforced trade show hours were from 8:00 a.m. to 6:00 p.m. Not everyone working in the booth was required to attend from start to finish, but *someone* had to man it during the trade show hours or pay a stiff fine.

Queenie motioned to the dark booth. "Today and tomorrow are usually the two busiest days of the market. He picked a helluva time not to show up."

I shrugged. "I dunno. Simon never misses an opportunity to get in front of a buyer. But he can't control traffic. Even if he were MIA, Lucinda would be in the booth. Sharon might have shut him down."

Queenie peeked into the booth. "Nope. The booth is still set up. All his samples and displays are ready for business."

I turned to face our booth. "Lucinda and Simon's two models are sitting in our booth. Let's ask them what's going on."

I walked in and put my messenger bag on one of the tables. "Good morning, team. How is everybody doing? Lauren and Lucinda, we missed you last evening. I hope everything is okay..."

Lucinda turned around, and my jaw dropped. An ugly black, purplish shiner ringed her right eye, swollen shut. The outline of a large hand was imprinted on her cheek. Her lower lip was swollen. Cuts, bruises, and scratches covered her arms.

I squatted in front of her to be at eye level and fought for control of my voice. "My Goddess. Were you in an accident?"

She hung her head and whispered so low that I had to lean my ear close to her lips to hear her. "I was attacked in the parking lot last night."

Tears dribbled down her cheeks and splashed onto my hands as my fingers raised her chin. "Luce, why are you here?"

She sniffled. "So as not to lose my job."

I said, "Simon's a jerk, but surely he doesn't expect you to work the booth looking like that." I grinned. "You might scare the customers away."

She laughed and grimaced as her swollen lips cracked. "I left a message on his cell phone, but he didn't return my call. This is a first. He's always opened up, especially during a market."

I traced my face and pointed to Lucinda's. "What happened?"

Lucinda said, "I dropped Jonathan off at my parents' house yesterday morning and ran late getting to work. By the time I arrived at the convention center, the front parking lot was full. The only parking still available was in the overflow lot that's in the rear of the convention center, across from the loading dock. I grabbed the last space in the last row and considered myself lucky. Before meeting the group for dinner, I told Lauren I wanted to lock my messenger bag in the trunk of my car so I didn't have to carry it around all evening."

I glanced at Lauren. "You didn't go with her?"

Lauren shrugged. "No. It wasn't dark, and plenty of people left the convention center—presumably going to the parking lots. The restaurant is in the opposite direction. I waited for Luce at the main entrance to the convention center. By the time dusk fell, she still hadn't returned, so I went to see if she was okay. The overflow lot butted up against a wooded area. I found Luce's car, but she wasn't in it. I figured we missed one another, and I started back to the lobby. I took out my cell phone and called her to stay put, or we'd keep missing each other. I realized something was wrong when a phone rang from the woods. Luce and I set a special ringtone on each other's phones so we'd always know it was the other one calling. I recognized her ringtone and ran back toward the woods. I screamed her name at the top of my lungs and kept running."

Lauren choked on a sob. "I-I guess I scared the guy off. I found her lying bruised and bloody behind some bushes. I checked her over and called nine-one-one."

I said, "So you never got a look at the guy?"

Lauren shook her head.

I turned to Lucinda. "Could you identify him? Was it someone familiar?"

She shook her head. "No. I opened the trunk, and he came up behind me. He never said a word the entire time. He put a gag in my mouth and dragged me into the woods. I was sure I was gonna die."

"Did he have a weapon?"

"He clamped one hand over my mouth, and an arm wrapped tight around my waist. He didn't have an available hand to hold a weapon, so I'd say no if asked to guess."

"See his face?"

"He wore a mask."

I scratched the crown of my head. "And no one in the parking lot noticed *anything*?"

Lucinda shook her head. "Every parking space was filled, but no one was in the parking lot. Everyone was going to dinner at restaurants within walking distance to the convention center so they could get back in time for the fashion show."

"Did he..." I couldn't bear to complete the sentence.

"N-no, thank God. I fought back. I got my fingers under the mask and scratched his face pretty badly, and he punched me in the eye. He let go of my arm to touch his face, and I kicked him in the balls. He punched me in the mouth and took off into the woods when Lauren yelled my name."

"Could you at least give the police a description of the guy's build?"

Lucinda hunched her shoulders. "Average height. Not skinny or fat."

"Young or old? Left or right-handed? Hair color? Short or long hair? Curly or straight? How was he dressed? The kind of shoes he wore? Clean-shaven or bearded? Any aftershave or cologne? Anything around his neck? Wear a watch or a ring?"

"I dunno. Lemme try to picture it." Lucinda rubbed her chin. "Light-colored pants and dark shoes." She sighed. "I was too scared to pay attention to details. The only thing I saw was a picture of Jonathan in my head. I focused on staying alive for him."

Lauren said, "The police arrived ten minutes later. Four patrolmen searched the woods and the area around the convention center, but they found no one. An ambulance took Luce to Miami Beach General. I arrived at the hospital at the same time as the police."

Lucinda said, "The doctor examined me first, and then a detective interviewed me."

Lauren snapped a pencil in half. "The detective wasn't too optimistic they'd ever catch the guy. At least Luce's pocketbook and her ID weren't taken."

"How long were you at the hospital?"

Lucinda looked at Lauren. "A couple of hours. The ER doctor stitched my lip, cleaned my shiner, as well as the cuts and bruises, and prescribed painkillers and antibiotics. He recommended I stay overnight for observation, but I declined, and he signed my release. The detective finished interviewing me, and Lauren took me home. She helped me clean up, got me into my pajamas, and put me to bed."

I turned to Lauren. "You stay with her?"

"No. I gave her the medications, waited until she was asleep, and went home. I wanted to stay, but she insisted she wanted to be alone."

I asked, "Was it a random act of opportunity or planned by someone familiar?"

Lucinda squeezed her eyes closed. "The detective asked me the same question. No one came to mind. Not my ex. Not an old boyfriend."

I tapped my lower lip. "The timing of the attack smacks of familiarity and not a random attack. Somebody followed you at that *specific time and on that particular day* because the parking lot had few people roaming around it due to the fashion show."

Luce shivered. "Who in the *swimwear business* is capable of such a vicious level of violence?"

I glanced across the hall at Simon's dark booth. *Nah. He's a bully, not a rapist. Or, if Lucinda turned down his demand to put out, maybe he's both. I wouldn't put it past him.*

I turned to Simon's models. "Ladies, are you independent or represented by an agency?"

A busty blonde answered, "Miami Mannequins Modeling Agency."

I said, "I'm going up to the Swimwear Association office. Come along. I'll confirm with your agency that you showed up for work and waited, but Simon never arrived. I'm sure he was required to pay an upfront cancellation fee when he signed the agency's contract. Ask Sharon if any vendors still need models. If she says there are, ask her to speak to your agency. They might be able to reassign you to another vendor."

I turned to the twins. "Lauren, take Luce home. Stay with her for the rest of the market. It's more important for you to take care of your sister than to be here." I swept a hand around the booth. "We have enough warm bodies to pick up the slack."

I motioned to Queenie. "Come on, partner. Let's go see Sharon."

Harriet said, "As long as you're going to the Swimwear office, do me a favor and stop off at the theater and pick up our samples. They'll be on a rack backstage in the sample storage room upstairs. The theater won't be open yet, but Sharon will give you the key."

I gave Harriet a thumbs-up, grabbed a canvas garment bag from the storage area, and then Queenie, the two models, and I left the booth.

Chapter Six

I glanced at Queenie as we made our way from the Swim Association office to the other side of the convention center. "What a weird meeting."

Queenie nodded. "I'll say. We laid out a strong case against Simon. *Anyone else* would have been banned from the trade show for life."

"According to Sharon, no other *vendor* made a formal complaint against Simon."

Queenie sniffed. "BS. Nancy Lookofsky called security to break up the fight between Simon and Walter Seiden so the rest of the vendors on the aisle could leave their booths."

I tsked. "And Sharon shrugged and said, '*Boys will be boys.*'"

Queenie asked, "Was Sharon being sarcastic by suggesting we go from booth to booth with a petition to ban Simon from future trade shows?"

I shook my head. "No. She was serious. If enough vendors signed the petition, then she'd have to take action."

Queenie pursed her lips. "No one died and left us in charge. If our competitors have a problem with Simon, let them open their mouths."

"The fastest way to get Simon banned is for *retailers* to complain to Sharon." I grinned. "I'll suggest it to my mother. She and Mariel will give Sharon an earful. By the time those two are done chewing her out, Sharon will *personally* pack up Simon's booth."

We walked through the lobby leading to the fashion theater. The staging company worked all night to break down the jungle and return the lobby to its original format.

I keyed the fashion theater door open. I felt around the inside wall for the panel of lights and switched them on. We crossed the threshold, and my nose twitched. "Phew. Something sure stinks. Do you smell it?"

"How could I miss it?" Queenie wrinkled her nose.

I grimaced. "Either the cleaning crew didn't empty the garbage containers, or a rat died."

Queenie shivered. "Let's not waste any time. I say we get the samples and scram."

I pinched my nose closed and pointed to the back of the theater. "The backstage door is on the left. Sharon said the sample storage room is up the first flight of stairs and is the last door on the right side."

The stairs creaked as we climbed up to the landing. Queenie took a whiff and held her nose. "Geez Louise, the stink is even stronger. Certainly not garbage. Something dead is rotting."

I opened the storage room door, and my eyes popped. The place was a wreck. Racks were turned over on their sides, and samples strewn helter-skelter all over the room.

I stared in disbelief. "The place looks as if a bomb hit it."

Queenie slapped her cheeks. "How the hell are we ever gonna find our samples in this mess?"

I walked halfway in and stopped short. I pointed across the room. "Something is dead, all right. And the rat is wearing khakis and loafers."

We tiptoed in for a closer look at the two long legs sticking out from under a pile of swimsuits. Simon Posnick's crumpled corpse lay spread-eagled and face down. His bloody head was turned at an unnatural angle, and the jagged edge of a coconut was embedded in the base of his skull.

Naturally, I burst out laughing.

Let's just say that genetics isn't all it's cracked up to be, and leave it there...

I gagged at the gore as I bent over Simon's skull, bashed in like a squashed pumpkin. I pointed at the fabric swatch attached to the edge of the coconut. "Queenie, look at the piece of torn fabric."

She glanced at it and shrugged. "From the look of this place, Simon put up a helluva fight. The shirt probably got ripped in the scuffle. It must have gotten caught on the edge of the coconut and embedded in his skull when the killer shoved the jagged edge into the back of Simon's head."

"Nope. *Take a closer look*. The piece of fabric is from *Mariel Levine's* silk shirt. Don't you remember? Mariel tried to get away from Simon last night, and her shirt was torn and stuck on the edge of the coconut when he tried to stop her from leaving."

Queenie smacked her forehead. "OMG! You're right." She gulped. "Is your mother's boss capable of doing something as gruesome as this?"

I've had a close relationship with Mariel Levine throughout my entire swimwear career. But suddenly, the possibility I might not know her at all was a punch in the gut that, if proven true, would break my heart and destroy my mother.

Chapter Seven

Nothing else could be done for Simon Posnick but call the police. While I spoke to the nine-one-one operator, Queenie called Harriet to bring her up to speed.

Ten minutes later, six Miami Beach PD uniforms and an EMT team arrived. A few years shy of retirement, Sergeant Solomon, a war-weary veteran of the mean streets whose hound dog sad brown eyes said he'd seen it all but never got used to it, was in charge. He asked for our ID, and we complied.

I indelicately snorted as one of the EMT team members slipped his hand into a surgical glove and checked Simon's pulse before confirming the victim was deceased. Was he for real? Even a blind guy could tell Simon Posnick was as dead as the proverbial doornail.

Solomon instructed two of the uniformed officers to clear the room, the theater, and the lobby. The sergeant directed another pair to frame the area surrounding Simon's corpse, the perimeter, and the interior of the storage room, with yellow crime scene tape.

Solomon separated Queenie and me. Fresh-faced Officer Bates questioned Queenie while Solomon interviewed me. When they finished, Solomon spoke into a microphone attached to the shoulder of his uniform shirt and called the scene into the station.

You could have knocked me over with a feather when, twenty minutes later, Miami Beach PD Homicide Detective *Moisés Lehrman* strode into the storage room. Moisés is the son of Abraham Lehrman, my dad's close friend and long-time customer. Mo and I were a hot item until I moved to California. Then the miles between us snuffed out our romance. Our nosy dads still cling to the hope that Mo and I will get back together.

I haven't seen Mo in four years. But he still can take my breath away. Six feet of solid muscle, with an olive complexion. He has two cute dimples that crease his cheeks when he smiles, and he still curls my toes. He sports a head of thick, brown, wavy hair my fingers beg to run through, and smoldering dark eyes I could easily get lost in. Damn him.

Mo opened his arms and raced toward me. But he glanced at Solomon and Queenie watching us with rapt interest, and stopped short and mumbled hello. Disappointment knotted my heartstrings. Yet I breathed a sigh of relief, unsure how I would have reacted if he had embraced me.

Mo held out a hand like a traffic cop as a sign for Queenie and me to stay put. Then he turned to confer with Solomon. The cop conference concluded, and the detective sidled over to Queenie and me. I introduced Queenie to Mo. He motioned for Queenie to join him on the far side of the room. My eyes had a mind of their own as they followed Mo crossing the room. Damn, the man still had a great tush.

Suddenly, the room temperature dropped fifty degrees, and a blast of icy cold air came out of nowhere and chilled me to the bone. I pulled my blazer tighter as two swirls of twin tornadoes emitted freezing air that spun counterclockwise. They whirred on either side of me and morphed into apparitions. The taller ghost was Marie LaValle, the late wife of Buddy LaValle, my current main squeeze. The smaller one was their deceased daughter, Justine. Good gravy. Either news traveled at warp speed in the Great Beyond, or my ghostly nemeses stalked me. Flip a coin.

Marie crossed her arms over her bodacious boobs and struck a menacing pose. She blew a blast of freezing air in my face to drive her ire home. Marie growled through clenched teeth, "Girlie, what in the Sam Hill is your problem? You're way past the expiration date for needin' a minder, but land sakes alive, ah cain't leave ya'll alone for a minute without them eyes of yours roaming to another man. Ya'll told mah Cajun boy ya'll were going to Miami, and Justine and I celebrated. Hallelujah! She's going to see her mama and commence working on the weddin' plans." Marie pointed an icicle-covered index finger at Mo. "We've been over this a few times already, but it's plain to see ya'll still need some remindin'. Ya'll cain't let another man come a courtin' since you're already promised to mah Buddy."

Justine hugged her teddy bear to her chest and stuck her lower lip out in an adorable pout. "Why don't you want to marry my daddy? He's such a nice man. He'll take good care of you the same way he did Mama and me."

Great. Another voice joined the chorus.

Marie swiped her frozen finger in front of her eyes. "Just remember, girlie...ah got mah eyes on you, so, you best stay on the straight and narrow."

The only person not on board with the let's get Holly hitched to Buddy concept is the prospective groom. The guy still wears his wedding band and has never even come close to proposing. Those two tidbits were immaterial to Buddy's ghostly family, who claimed they couldn't move on to their final resting place until they were certain that Buddy would not live his life all alone. But if and when he pops the question, a wedding will be on our timeframe and not up to his late wife and child.

Before I telepathically explained to Marie LaValle in *vivid detail the exact place she could shove her wedding plans,* Mo sidled next to me, and the two ghosts disappeared into thin air.

Mo gave me the once-over with concerned eyes. "Are you okay? You look as if you've seen a ghost."

Two, but who's counting...

Chapter Eight

I convinced Mo that, considering the circumstances, I was fine, and he reluctantly agreed to conduct my interview. My heart melted as he smiled and brushed his fingertips across my cheek. "I hate the circumstances that brought us together, but it's still so good to see you."

I giggled and made finger quotes in the air. "Wait until the daddios get wind of *our reunion*...then the fun and games will begin."

Mo dipped his head. "Would a *reunion* be such a bad thing?"

Oh boy. Would it? My heart jackhammered in my ears. Yes. No. Maybe. How the hell do I know? Ten minutes ago, a reunion with Moisés Lehrman was the last thing on my mind. I mentally pulled my head out of the past and shoved it back into the present. What the hell was I thinking? A LAPD captain *dumped me* not long ago. So, I needed another cop in my life as much as a bigger tush. And if we resumed our love affair? What do I do about Buddy LaValle? And if all that wasn't enough to throw a bucket of cold water on the concept, let's face it, long-distance relationships are destined to end in heartbreak. The how-and-ifs alone of the prospect made me dizzy.

He didn't wait for my response. Then, as though a curtain fell at the end of an act in a play, a veil shrouded his expression, and Detective Lehrman was all business. Maybe he was afraid to hear my answer...no kidding...he wasn't the only one.

Mo pulled a nub of a pencil and a dog-eared spiral notepad from his back pocket and flipped the spiral open to a blank page. "You called the incident in?"

"Yes."

He angled his head to Simon's supine corpse. "Do you know the deceased?"

"Yes."

"What's his name?"

"Simon Posnick."

Mo scribbled a note and looked up. "What, if any, is your relationship with Mr. Posnick?"

"We're competitors. His booth is across from ours at the swimwear trade show in the convention center."

Mo swept an arm around the room. "Why were you and Ms. Levine in this room?"

I pointed to the piles of samples scattered around the room. "Our samples were featured in the theater's fashion show last night. We came to get them."

"Was Mr. Posnick here for the same reason?"

I shrugged. "No idea." I pointed to Simon's corpse. "We found him exactly as you see him."

Mo eyed the mountains of samples. "How many suppliers participated in the fashion show?"

I scrunched my eyes closed in concentration. "The program guide listed fifty vendors."

"Do you know what the seating capacity of the fashion theater is?"

I shook my head. "No, but it was a full house."

Mo tapped his lower lip with the pencil's eraser. "How did you get into the building today?"

I dangled the key. "Sharon Gold is the Swimwear Association Director. She gave me the key."

He said, "All fashion show attendees must be interviewed, everyone from the models to the make-up artists, the guests, the workers, bartenders, and vendors. Do you know if Ms. Gold can supply all the contact information?"

I nodded. "Yes. She has the theater seating capacity information, a printout of all the vendors and supplier participants, and a list of all ticketed guests."

Mo made a note and angled his head at the storage room door. "Was the door open?"

"It was closed but unlocked."

Mo shot the questions out in a rat-a-tat-tat staccato of a pistol. "Move the victim or check his pulse? Touch any garments or move any to find your samples?"

"No. The only thing I did was call nine-one-one."

He took notice of every inch of the destroyed storage room and scratched a few lines on the notepad. "Our victim put up a helluva fight."

Nothing gets past you, Sherlock.

He pointed to the jagged edge of the coconut embedded in the base of Simon's skull and shook his head. "Only in Miami."

Bet me, bucko. If coconuts grew on LA palm trees, one would definitely end up as a murder weapon. And naturally, I'd be the lucky one to discover the crime scene.

Mo raised the crime scene tape and squatted under it. He scooted closer to the corpse and studied it from every angle. "The piece of fabric impaled on the edge of the coconut isn't from anything the victim is wearing." He leaned over the fabric swatch for a closer examination. "I'm no fashion expert, but it looks like it's from a woman's garment. Is it from a sample?"

I shrugged.

He arched a brow. "Or...our killer is a woman."

He narrowed his eyes. "Do you recognize the fabric?"

Crap on a crumpet.

My worst fear came to fruition.

I owed my swimwear career to Mariel Levine. I'd do almost anything for her...except lie to the police. Especially to this particular cop who could spot my lying face almost as fast as my mother.

As I opened my mouth to answer, the storage room door opened, and the Assistant Dade County Coroner, as well as the medical examiner's and CSI teams, arrived carrying a gurney and a large assortment of crime scene paraphernalia. The motley group danced their way into the festivities in the corpse-cutter conga line that was all too familiar to a murder magnet like me.

They were decked out in crime-scene protective clothing—a full-body suit, a hood, a mask dangling on a strap around their necks, booties, and gloves. I broke into a sweat just looking at them. It was a miracle they didn't melt into puddles while schlepping all their equipment in eighty-degree heat and ninety percent humidity while wearing those get-ups.

Mo grinned when Doctor Jasmine Jones entered the room. "Dr. J., long time no see."

Dr. Jones' throaty voice rumbled in a deep timbre reminiscent of Lauren Bacall. "I'm the right color," she feigned shooting a basketball into an imaginary hoop, "but not nearly tall enough to be called Dr. J."

On the shady side of her mid-thirties, Assistant Medical Examiner Jasmine Jones' eyes were the most gorgeous chocolate brown imaginable. She had a beaming smile and a mouth full of straight, dazzling white choppers.

I eyed her standing at around five-six and one hundred and thirty pounds. Muscular with the toned physique of an active lifestyle, yet everything about her exuded femininity. Her flawless skin was an ochre color, the way mellow-brown light bathes the forest.

Mo turned to Queenie and me and did the introductions. "JJ, Ms. Levine and Ms. Schlivnik discovered the victim's body and called it in."

I smiled and touched Queenie's arm. "Please call me Holly, and my business partner is Queenie."

Dr. Jones' dry handshake was firm and decisive. She gave each of our hands a quick squeeze and released them. "Nice to meet you both. Please call me Jazzy."

She motioned to Simon and grinned. "I love my job. My patients never complain or self-diagnose."

I burst out laughing. "I have a close friend back home in LA who is an assistant medical examiner, and she says the same thing."

Dr. Jones narrowed her eyes. "I'm originally from California and friendly with many of the LA County medical examiners. May I ask your friend's name?"

"Sophie Cutler."

Dr. Jones squeaked as loudly as a new pair of patent leather shoes. "*Sophie Cutler? Get out of town, girl!* We went through UC Berkeley-UCSF Medical School together. Sophie, Sherry Silverman, and I were as tight as ticks in a blanket. Isn't it a small world? Have you been friends with her for a long time?"

I nodded. "Yep. Snip and I have been BFFs ever since fate put us together as lab partners in Mr. Hepburn's seventh-grade biology class."

Jazzy looked at me oddly. "Why do you call her *Snip*?"

I said, "Frog dissection made me queasy, and Sophie was incapable of composing a decent essay. So, we struck a win-win deal. I wrote her compositions, and she dissected my frog. That's why Snip is her nickname."

Jazzy tapped her cheeks and laughed. "Wait until I call Sophie. Won't she be surprised you and I met, especially under these circumstances?"

I smiled at the irony. "She won't be. This isn't my first rodeo. Regrettably, Simon Posnick's corpse wasn't the first one I ever discovered."

Jazzy blinked with surprise. "*It wasn't*?"

Queenie smirked. "Nope. Not by a long shot." Queenie cuffed my bicep. " Hol, tell Jazzy LAPD's nickname for you."

"I'd rather not..."

Jazzy waggled her fingers. "Come on, no need to be shy..."

I sighed. "We work in the California Apparel Mart. I discovered several murders that took place in the building..." I rolled my eyes. "A wise-ass homicide detective on one of the cases nicknamed me Triple M..."

Helpful Queenie chimed in, "Which stands for the *Mart Murder Magnet*."

Jazzy widened her eyes. "How many murders are we talking about?"

Queenie counted them on her fingers. "Five...*so far*."

Jazzy slapped her cheeks. "Man, when they say *killer clothes*, they aren't kidding...Who knew the rag business was so lethal?"

I grinned. "What can I say? It's a gift."

But Queenie wasn't finished. "Holly is too humble to tell you not only has she discovered several murder victims, but when the police arrested the wrong suspect, she investigated on her own, identified the real killers, and solved the crimes for the police."

Mo's jaw dropped. "You *interfered* with *active* police murder investigations? It may be okay in LA, but in Miami Beach, interference in a police investigation is a *serious crime*."

I pursed my lips. "If you conduct a thorough investigation and arrest the right suspect, then there's no reason for me to investigate."

I shrugged. "If not, all bets are off..."

Mo pointed his index finger and thumb shaped like a pistol at my heart. "Do not think for a nanosecond that our relationship gives you any sway. If you interfere in this case in any way, I will not hesitate to arrest you for interference in an official, active police homicide investigation."

I smiled sweetly. "It all comes down to the two Cs. Confidence and competence."

Chapter Nine

Despite an emotionally tense, seemingly endless day, I spent a restless night tossing and turning and having disturbing dreams that woke me shaken and drenched in sweat.

I gave up on getting any decent sleep before the first inkling of dawn. I threw on shorts, a tank top, and laced up my sneakers.

I took the elevator down to the lobby and exited from the hotel's rear entrance. I headed for the beach and a stroll on the boardwalk to clear the cobwebs out of my addled brain.

The lower lip of a tangerine sun barely settled onto the eastern horizon as night ceded time to day, but it was already a toasty eighty-five degrees. Damp fingers of humidity curled over the wooden boardwalk, giving the briny sea air a mushy texture.

Still logy from my sleep-deprived night, I stopped at the takeaway window at the beachside entrance of Brews & Bagels. I ordered an extra-large cuppa to-go, strong enough to strip the paint off my houseboat. The temperature inched higher by the minute. This was a dandy time to test the odd-sounding old wives' tale my mother swears by, that to cool off in hot, muggy weather, drink hot, not cold, beverages.

Four healthy gulps later, I wasn't any cooler. Rivulets of perspiration poured from my hairline to my face, and fat drops rolled off the tip of my nose. It didn't cool me off, but the jolt of java dissolved the cobwebs clogging my brain and gave me a fighting chance to make some sense of yesterday.

It was too early for the throngs of sunbathers who usually packed the beach, so the boardwalk was all mine as I strolled parallel to the ocean. The Atlantic's pristine water was a stunning mixture of royal blue and turquoise. I stared, mesmerized by the calm waters that glistened under the sun. The dazzling white sand of the shoreline framed the ocean like a painting in a museum, enhancing the water's beauty.

I walked to the end of the pier and sat on a wooden bench facing the ocean. I watched an old guy cast and recast a line. His tanned face, leathery from exposure to the relentless sun, reminded me of Pop, the senior citizen fisherman I befriended on the Washington Street pier at home.

Despite my attempts to stop it, my mind wandered back to the scene of the crime.

Who impaled the back of Simon's head with the coconut?

Is Mariel capable of murder?

If not her, who?

What do I do about Mo?

What do I want to do about Mo?

What should I do about Mo?

What about Buddy?

What do I want to do about Buddy?

What should I do about Buddy?

What do I say to my mother about all this?

Anything?

Something?

Everything?

Nothing?

My head asked questions that my heart had no answers to.

Lucky me.

I tossed the to-go cup into the trash container and squared my shoulders. It was time to shake things up, kick some ass, and take numbers. And get those questions answered before they drive me mad.

Chapter Ten

After a shower and a change of clothes, I took the elevator down to the lobby and headed for the newsstand. The boldface headline above the fold on the *East Coast Apparel News* read: *Swim Show Stunner: Rep Impaled By Coconut.*

Our motley crew arrived at our regular table at the back of Brews & Bagels at seven-thirty on the nose. I laid the paper headline face up on the center of the table. The Yentas' mood was subdued as Queenie and I recounted the gruesome discovery of Simon's body and the ensuing events of the day.

I deadpanned to lighten things up, "Well, the good news is there's no danger of Simon as a neighbor at the next market..."

Joan pursed her lips. "It all worked out pretty well for everyone but Simon..."

Hope grimaced as she tapped a teaspoon on the newspaper headline. "The back of his head was *impaled* by the jagged edge of a *coconut shell*?"

Queenie nodded. "Yes, ma'am."

Joan pursed her lips. "Eek. Head wounds are so bloody."

Sonia gave me the once-over and smirked. "So, you laughed?"

No point denying it. My reputation preceded me.

Besides, even if I wanted to, Queenie was a witness.

I rolled my eyes. "You need to ask?"

Hope surveyed the table. "So, who killed Simon?"

Queenie tapped her index finger on the tip of her nose. "On TV, the detectives always say to follow the money. Who has the most to lose?"

I sighed. "I hate to say it, but the obvious one is Mariel Levine. She and Simon had a nasty public confrontation the night of the fashion show. The fabric swatch pinned to the coconut shell is from *her blouse.* The *physical evidence* ties her to the crime."

Sonia bit her lower lip. "Does the detective know the fabric swatch is from Mariel's blouse?"

"He does." I hung my head. "He asked me if I recognized the fabric swatch, and as much as I hated to point him in Mariel's direction, I couldn't lie. I owe Mariel my swimwear career..."

Hope tipped her head to the side. "How?"

I answered, "When I worked for my father, he was interviewed for the Ditzy Swimwear Southeast territory job. Rob Bachmann, the Ditzy owner, was reluctant to hire Dad because of *me*."

Joan asked, "He knew you?"

I shook my head. "No, it wasn't personal. He was against hiring a *woman*."

Sonia gave me the big eyes. "Why?"

I dipped my head. "He was concerned that he'd spend the time and energy to train *a girl*, and then she'd meet a guy, get married, and quit traveling on the road."

Joan smacked her palm on the table hard enough to spill her coffee. "The rotten chauvinist pig!"

Sonia asked, "What was Mariel's part?"

"Laurie's was Ditzy's largest volume Florida account and in the top five for the country." I grinned. "Mariel told Rob if he was too stupid not to hire *that kid*, he was too stupid to sell to Laurie's." I held out my hands in supplication. "I would do anything for Mariel...except lie to the police."

I steepled my fingers. "With all the trouble Simon caused Mariel, I couldn't blame her if she killed him, but in my heart of hearts...nah. Mariel said Simon's big threat to use against her was nothing more than hot air. Her reputation in the industry is stellar, so I believe her."

Hope patted my arm. "You did the right thing. And if she is innocent, Mariel will agree."

I nodded. "She is, and she will. But I owe her at least a heads-up that she's probably Mo's number one suspect."

Joan never misses a nuance. "*Mo*? *You and the cop are already on a first-name basis*?" She puckered her lips. "What *is it with you and* police detectives? No sooner is one cop out of your life than another one takes his place."

"My dad and Abraham Lehrman, Moisés' father, are BFFs who share a love of backgammon, cigars, and Jai-Lai. Mo and I met through our fathers when he was the Chief Financial Officer of his father's chain of women's apparel stores. The retail business wasn't his cup of tea, so Mo resigned to enter the police academy a few years before I moved back to LA."

Sonia widened her eyes. "Boy, talk about a huge career change."

I nodded. "It was. He wanted to do something to show his gratitude for how Miami welcomed him and his family when they arrived as refugees."

Hope asked, "Where are they from originally?"

"The Lehrmans are Jubanos."

Joan asked, "And a Jubano is?"

"A Cuban Jew. They bribed a fisherman to take them to Key West on a moonless night. They hid beneath the deck in the boat's hold and drugged the children so they'd stay quiet if the Cuban Coast Guard stopped the boat. They reached the shores of Key West in the middle of the night and were met by a Miami-based refugee organization."

Joan pointed to the other Yentas. "We've been meeting every weekday morning for coffee for a few years now." She scrunched her face into an annoyed kindergarten teacher frown. "And yet, this is the first time we're hearing about this man. What's the story? He's got warts or something?"

I pursed my lips. "Mo and I were quite close until I moved back to California. I hadn't seen, spoken to, or thought about Mo in years. His arrival at the crime scene as the homicide detective was a real surprise. Until now, it was a closed chapter in my life, so there was no story to tell."

Always to the point, Sonia asked, "And if he wants to resume the relationship? Do you want him back in your life?"

I shrugged.

Hope tossed her fifty-cents worth into the pot. "What about Buddy?"

What about Buddy, indeed...

And as if this situation wasn't already complicated enough, my two favorite ghosts are busy sticking their noses into the hot mess. Of course, I didn't include the apparitions in my story. Why add the woo-woo to the mix? The real story was already crazy enough.

I held out my hands. "And now? I'm not sure. Mo and I are having dinner tomorrow night. I'll see if there's still smoke and a fire."

Nana's warning whispered inside my head. "*Don't start something you're not prepared to see through.*"

Queenie reminded me of my nana when she tapped her index finger on the tip of her nose. "If you play with fire, chances are you're gonna get burned."

Chapter Eleven

There was only *one* topic of discussion at the convention center. The news of Simon Posnick's murder raced through the complex like a speeding rocket. We approached our booth, and I shivered at the sight of yellow crime scene tape draped across Simon Posnick's dark booth like a tie binding a shroud.

Next, will the Grim Reaper be our booth greeter?

Harriet and Lauren were both working when we walked into our booth.

Queenie nudged me. "It's a good thing Lauren came in to help Harriet, but I'm kind of surprised to see her."

I smiled. "Either Lucinda's recovery was a swift one, or she drove her sister nuts."

Just then, four groups of retailers arrived. It was a full house with every station occupied. All hands were on deck for the next three hours.

I sidled over to Lauren when the rush subsided. "Queenie and I were surprised to see you here. Is Luce doing better?"

Lauren shrugged. "It's hard to say if she's doing better or enjoys being a drama queen. She went into her Greta Garbo routine and said, '*I vant to be alone*.' So, I granted her wish and hightailed it out of her house before she changed her mind." Lauren rolled her eyes. "Let's just say, Luce is not a great patient..."

I grinned. "She was driving you crazy, right?"

Lauren fanned her face. "You have no idea."

Three chimes from a recorded xylophone broadcast over the loudspeaker. "*Your attention, please. This is Sharon Gold, Florida Swimwear Association Director. Moisés Lehrman, the MBPD lead homicide detective assigned to investigate the tragic murder of our own Simon Posnick, has requested to address all attendees. Please give him your undivided attention."*

Mo cleared his throat and began. "*Thank you, Ms. Gold. The Swimwear Association has provided my team with a printout of all vendors and suppliers participating in the trade show, a list of all registered retailers, and a list of names and contact information for all ticketed attendees of the fashion show. MBPD must interview everyone on those lists. Given the volume of people, we assembled interview teams to conduct the meetings. To facilitate scheduling, six team members are posted at each convention center exit. To leave the building, you must present your photo ID, proof of registration, and schedule an interview time."*

A universal groan echoed through the convention center's main arena.

"*We understand that time-sensitive business is being conducted. We will be as unobtrusive as possible. We have allotted fifteen minutes for each interview, with the caveat that a follow-up meeting will be scheduled if necessary. The Convention Center management has made its conference rooms available for our interviews. They have extended the open hours until nine p.m. We will register and schedule all interviewees today. All interviews will be conducted tomorrow, from seven a.m. through nine p.m. Your scheduled interview time will be entered into the police computer. These interviews are mandatory. Failure to appear will be considered the same as a failure to appear in court for a subpoena. A marshal will be sent to your booth, hotel, home, or store to escort you to your interview. Your cooperation is imperative to complete all interviews and for us to gather as much information as possible to apprehend the perpetrator of this heinous crime. If everyone on these lists is not registered and interviewed, we will declare the convention center complex a crime scene and close the entire place down. This is not a threat. It is a promise. The interview registration teams are set up. The MBPD appreciates your cooperation."*

I faced our group. "Give Lauren your police interview time to ensure all customer meetings are covered." I pointed to the aisle. "Let's get these interviews scheduled ASAP. Lauren, I will tell Detective Lehrman that you will schedule Luce's interview. Harriet, leave two models and two sales reps in the booth to cover the appointments. Everyone else, go to the south exit and get your interview scheduled."

My mother called an hour later with a list of samples for a style-out the next day. I was having dinner with my mother, so I said I'd bring the samples to her office, and we could leave for dinner together.

Lauren packed the samples, a line list, and a set of swatch cards into a canvas garment bag. I left early to comply with the MBPD requirement. Avril Wilts finished registering in the line next to me and tapped me on the shoulder.

Avril pointed to my pass. "What time is your interview? Mine is at seven a.m. Even God isn't up *that* early!"

"Be happy that yours is the earliest appointment."

She scowled. "I'm not a morning person. Are you?"

I nodded. "Yeah, I am. I live at the beach in Marina del Rey. Each morning before sunrise, my dog and I walk from our houseboat to the Washington Street pier and back."

She rolled her eyes. "The only sunrise I want to experience is a Tequila Sunrise. Do you walk in the morning while you're at the market, too?"

"Yes. I'm a creature of habit."

"Since you're going to be up before the crack of dawn anyway, let's swap times. Yours must be later than mine."

I shook my head. "Sorry. No can do. I've already been interviewed."

"How? The interview registration just started."

"I discovered Simon's corpse. The cops questioned me for hours."

She patted her cheeks. "You found *another dead body*? Geesh, you're not called Triple M for nothing."

Another voice joins the chorus.

My reputation is now nationwide.

Probably viral over the internet by now.

Billboard announcements along the interstates are next.

Lucky me.

I crossed my heart. "I am blessed."

I checked the time. "Listen, I'd love to stay and chat," I said, shifting the garment bag to my right arm. "But I've gotta get these samples delivered for a style out tomorrow."

She eyed the garment bag as warily as a ticking bomb. "Who conducts a style out before the market is over?"

None of your business.

Right.

Good luck, Schlivnik.

This ought to be fun. If your idea of an enjoyable time is a tooth extraction.

"The advertising team at Laurie's."

She growled through clenched teeth, "That bitch will get hers someday."

Chapter Twelve

I resisted the urge to run and counted the lucky stars that I managed to escape Avril's ire. I exited the convention center into the sweltering humidity and sweated off five pounds while standing in the cab line. A dusty, late-model German luxury sedan with a lit roof sign advertising *Tyrell's Taxi* was the last cab. Beggars, especially ones melting by the minute, can't be choosers. So, I opened the back door and slid in. Crap. All the windows were open, but the interior temperature was as hot as an oven. No air conditioning. Just an ineffective fan on the dashboard whirring the sticky air around.

A middle-aged black man with an Afro haircut turned halfway around in the driver's seat to face me. A diamond in his front tooth caught the sunlight when he smiled. He spoke formally, but in a sing-song accent typical of Trinidad. "Good day, madam. Do you prefer Mother Nature's air conditioning or the manmade, artificial variety?"

My lungs on fire, I choked out, "AC, please."

He said, "Very good, madam." He leaned over the dashboard and flipped the AC switch on. From the way it coughed and sputtered, the last time it was turned on was probably before the cabbie was in long pants.

He looked into the rearview mirror. "I'll leave the windows open and the fan on until the air conditioner gets cold."

Fanfreakingtastic. We'd be in Jacksonville by then. Thank the Goddess Laurie's executive office wasn't far from the convention center.

I gave the driver Laurie's Fashions' address. He raised the meter arm, made a U-turn, and pulled out of the convention center parking lot into bumper-to-bumper traffic on A1A northbound.

I smacked my fist into my palm. "Dammit, I figured it was early enough to beat the rush hour traffic."

He glanced in the rearview mirror and said, "Not to worry, madam, I'll take the back way, and you will arrive on time."

Back way?

He pulled into the first left turn lane and cut off a southbound bobtail truck. He sped across the two lanes of oncoming traffic just as the traffic light changed from red to green. I closed my eyes and clung to the armrest. The famous chase scene from The French Connection played in my mind. Red warning lights signaled that a bridge was about to open. We crossed the drawbridge over the Intracoastal Waterway seconds before the gate closed and the bascule bridge opened into an inverted V, letting an oversized yacht pass through.

Half a mile due west, we turned north onto Breeze Blvd, which paralleled A1A. Five miles later, my heart slowed from a thumping bass drum and returned to a normal thud as we turned east on Bayside Avenue and made another right onto A1A southbound. The Lauries' corporate office was two traffic lights down the road on the same side of the street.

We pulled up to the main entrance, and Tyrell's version of Mr. Toad's Wild Ride concluded remarkably scratch-free as the taxi lurched to a stop. Tyrell pushed the meter arm down and turned around. His diamond-studded tooth glinted in the sunlight as he turned his head facing west to look at me. "The fare is fourteen dollars and twenty-five cents. I accept credit cards, but not checks. If you can pay in cash, it will be greatly appreciated."

I handed him a twenty. I told him to keep the change, and he almost leaped over the seat to hug me.

I said, "No worries. You earned it. You made it in..." I searched for the right words. "Record-breaking time, and I appreciate it."

He snatched the twenty out of my hand before I changed my mind. He handed me a business card and said to call him if I ever need another ride.

Right. You'll be the first one I call if I have a death wish.

Chapter Thirteen

The receptionist called my mother and handed me a visitor's badge to clip onto my shirt. Mom opened the door to the executive offices and beckoned me in. I followed her down a long, narrow hallway.

I peeked into Mariel's vacant big office, attached by an open breezeway door to Mom's smaller office. I clucked my tongue in disappointment. "Geez, you said Mariel was in the office. Is she gone for the day or in a meeting? If she's still in the building, I need to speak to her regarding the presentation."

Mom made a funny face and leaned closer to speak in a low, conspiratorial voice. "She is here. A minute after I hung up with you, Mo Lehrman called and asked to speak to Mariel. I said she was in a meeting. He said he was on his way over and for her to be available to answer questions." Mom sighed, and my heart sank to my toes. "It's a good thing you called and prepped her. He arrived ten minutes before you. They just went into the conference room down the hall."

I asked, "Is the conference room door open or closed?"

Mom shrugged. "I dunno."

I gave her a come-on wave. "Only one way to find out. Lead the way."

Mom's eyes widened. "Why?"

I smirked. " Mo and I are having dinner tomorrow night, and I want to tell him I've got a yen for Chinese food." I rolled my eyes. "*Why do you think*? If the door is open, to eavesdrop on the interrogation."

Mom stuck her tongue out. "Okay, Miss Smarty Pants. Follow me."

I left the presentation in Mom's office, and we tiptoed down the hall, slinking close to the walls like a couple of second-story burglars. Mom stopped in front of the last room on the right side and made a ta-da motion. Hot diggity, the door was miraculously half open.

Mo said, "I appreciate your taking the time to see me, Ms. Levine."

Was she given a choice?

I whispered into Mom's ear. "Go back into your office. If you're not here and I get caught, you'll have plausible deniability when Mo interviews you."

Mom whispered back, "Okay, but won't Mo be furious if he catches you eavesdropping?"

I waved the idea away. "Nah. If I get caught, I'll say I got lost on the way to the ladies' room and stopped to ask for directions. Mo has no idea if I've been to the Laurie's office before or not."

I shooed her away to skedaddle. Mom squeezed my shoulder and said, "Be careful." Then she scampered down the hallway and disappeared into her office. I plastered my body perpendicular to the outside wall at the conference room entrance so I could see in, but not be seen. Mo sat across from Mariel at a large conference room table.

Mo took a small notepad and a stub of a pencil from his inside jacket pocket. He pointed to the swimsuit samples hung on a grid on the back wall. "I can see you are busy, so I'll try not to take too much of your time."

Mariel nodded, and Mo flipped the notebook to a clean page. He poised the pencil, ready to write. "You knew Mr. Posnick?"

"Yes."

"How?"

"He was a rep."

"You had a relationship with the victim?"

"Yes."

Mo jotted a note and looked up. "In what capacity?"

Mariel raised her brows and smiled as she pointed to the swimsuit samples on the grid. "Well, Detective Lehrman, I said he was a rep..."

I internally cheered. *Good on you, Mariel! Never let a wiseass cop get away with playing stupid games.*

The annoyed expression on Mo's face said Mariel would pay a price for her indulgence.

Mo pointed to the swimsuits hung on plastic display forms. "I understand that he was a rep, Ms. Levine. However, for all I know, Mr. Posnick sold you the *display forms*. So do us both a favor. Please quit jerking me around and *answer the question*."

Mariel smiled sweetly. "I thought I answered it already. For your clarification, Simon was the *swimwear sales rep* for one of the lines I buy from."

"Was your relationship with him a long one, or was it new?"

"Almost as long as I've been a buyer at Laurie's."

Mo looked up and smiled. "At the risk of intruding on your age, how many years are we talking about?"

Mariel looked Mo up and down and laughed out loud. "Detective, I've been a buyer here since the time you attended high school."

"So, you knew him well?"

"If you're asking if we ever broke bread together, the answer is no."

"So, only in a professional capacity."

"Yes. If I bought a line he represented, he was the sales rep I dealt with."

Mo tapped the pencil eraser on the edge of the table. "How would you characterize your relationship with Mr. Posnick?"

Mariel pursed her lips. "It had its ups and downs."

"Meaning?"

"Meaning the relationship between reps and retailers is a naturally adversarial one. "

"In what respect?"

Mariel smiled sardonically. "Well, it's kind of like the weather. If you're planning a day at the beach and the forecast calls for it to pour all day, you're gonna be disappointed. If the forecast calls for a sunny day, you're gonna do the happy dance."

Mo held up his wrist and tapped the face of his watch. "Ms. Levine, I have neither the time nor the inclination to go to Cleveland by way of Cairo, trying to get a straight answer out of you. So, can the wiseass analogies and get to the point."

Mariel sighed. "Okay, Detective. Let me give you the bottom line. If I wrote a size order that, *in Simon's opinion,* his line warranted, the relationship was all lollipops and roses. If not, the relationship turned adversarial."

"How?"

"His line was a significant percentage of many retailers' assortments, including ours. It didn't matter if his product warranted it or not. Simon threw his weight around for more floor space and a larger share of a buyer's open-to-buy. Intimidation and threats of going over a buyer's head to management weren't beneath him."

Mo arched a brow. "And the word on the street is he used those tactics on you."

Mariel shrugged her dismissal. "Let's not go in..."

Mo held up a hand. "Don't even try to deny it, Ms. Levine. Several people standing next to you and the victim in the theater lobby the night of the fashion show witnessed a rather nasty altercation between the two of you. Mr. Posnick threatened you with extortion, ruining your reputation, and getting you fired if you did not meet his demands."

Mo lifted a case marked *Evidence* up from the floor and placed it on the table. He took a pair of surgical gloves out of his jacket pocket and slipped them on. He opened the case, removed a towel, and spread it on the table. Mo pulled a clear plastic container from the case containing the bloody coconut shell and placed it on the towel.

Mo turned the plastic container around so the bloody jagged edge faced her. He pushed the container closer to Mariel. She gasped when the blood-soaked fabric swatch was only inches away from her nose. Mo tapped the pencil's eraser on the container. "Do you recognize this, Ms. Levine?"

Mariel leaned closer and examined the coconut shell from every angle. "It looks the same as the coconut shell I drank a Batida de Coco from the night of the fashion show."

Mo mocked her. "It *looks* the same as, Ms. Levine? You're not *positive*?" Mo tapped the container in the spot where the fabric swatch was caught on the coconut shell. "See anything familiar?"

Mariel studied the container as though it held the secret of life.

Mo's booming voice rattled the windows. "*Well, Ms. Levine.*" He slammed his hand on the table so hard that the plastic container slid across into Mariel's hands. "*Is it or is it not the coconut you drank from*?"

Mariel pushed the container away as if it had cooties. "It is the coconut shell I drank from." She blinked with surprise as if seeing the coconut shell for the first time. "But, how did it get soaked in blood?" She held her hands up and turned them around to face Mo. "I didn't cut myself the night of the fashion show, nor any before or since."

Mo curled his upper lip. "Come on now, Ms. Levine, don't play dumb. You know the answers to those questions only too well."

Mariel's back stiffened. "Detective Lehrman, I have no idea what you're talking about. The last time I touched that coconut shell was in the fashion theater lobby. I finished my drink and threw it into a trash container." She jutted her jaw. "And let me assure you, as I tossed it into the trash container, *not a drop of blood, mine or anyone else's*, was on that coconut shell. How the coconut shell got soaked in blood is a mystery to me. If you don't believe me, ask the people I was with. In addition to Natalie Schlivnik, Avril Wilts, the sales rep for Tigress Swimwear, and her bosses were there."

Mo grunted and changed course. He pointed to the fabric swatch. "Do you recognize the piece of fabric?"

Mariel nodded. "Yes."

"Who does it belong to?"

Mariel tapped her right index finger into her cleavage. "Me. It's from the sleeve of the silk blouse I wore the night of the fashion show."

"How did it get impaled onto the edge of the coconut?"

Mariel said, "As you stated earlier, Simon and I exchanged words before the fashion show started. When I'd said everything I had to say, I told him that our conversation was over. However, Simon disagreed and insisted that our discussion wasn't finished. When I tried to leave the lobby and enter the theater, he blocked my way." Mariel held up her arm to demonstrate. "He grabbed my arm, and I pulled it away, but part of the sleeve caught on the jagged edge of the coconut I held in my other hand. A piece of the fabric ripped off and snagged onto the coconut shell." Mariel clucked her tongue. "The big ape ruined a hundred-and-fifty-dollar silk blouse and made no apology, let alone an offer to replace it."

Mo asked, "And then?"

Mariel smiled evilly. "And then I told him if he didn't get out of the way, he'd never see another order from Laurie's."

"Did he comply?"

"I didn't give him the chance to decide yes or no." Mariel huffed righteously. "I took Natalie by the arm and sidestepped the jerk, and we went inside the theater."

"When did you see him next?"

"There was no next time."

"Didn't run into him at intermission or after the fashion show ended?"

"No."

Mo cocked a brow. "Well, he didn't disappear into thin air. If he wasn't in the theater or the lobby, where was he?"

Mariel shrugged. “I have no idea. The theater lobby was packed to capacity. We could have been ten feet apart and not seen one another. He could have been in the men’s room or left the building before the fashion show ended to avoid the crowd and been halfway home by the time it let out.”

Mo asked, “Where did you go after the fashion show?”

Mariel looked at him oddly. “Home. Where else would I go?”

“You and Natalie Schlivnik or the others didn’t go out for coffee?”

Mariel shook her head. “Natalie was meeting Holly. I don’t know Avril and her bosses well enough to socialize with them. And even if we were friends, I was too tired to go anywhere but home. We’d worked all day, and the fashion show wasn’t over until ten o’clock. All I wanted to do was get home, take a bath, and go to bed. Natalie waited for Holly as they had plans. So, I said good night to the group and left.”

“Ms. Wilts and her management were still in the theater lobby when you say you left?”

Mariel nodded.

“Speak to anyone in the parking lot? Did anyone see you get into your car or see you drive away?”

Mariel shook her head.

“Make any stops on the way home? Put gas in the car? Drive through a fast-food line or go inside and grab a burger? Stop at a twenty-four-hour market to pick up a quart of milk?”

Mariel blew the air out of her cheeks. “Detective, I speak perfect English. Which part of I *went straight home* do you not understand?”

Mo opted to ignore Mariel’s sarcasm. “What time did you get home?”

She scrunched her eyes in concentration. “Around ten-forty-five.”

Mo asked, “Anyone home?”

“My husband.”

“Did you speak to him?”

Mariel swatted the question away as though it were an unwelcome fly at a picnic. "Nah. Murray was snoring as loudly as a freight train, and I was thrilled. It had been a long, tiring day. I was in no mood for any conversation. As I said before, all I wanted was to soak in a hot bath and to sink my weary bones into bed."

Mo smiled, but the smile never made it to his eyes. "Since you didn't see or speak to anyone, no one can confirm your whereabouts, activities, or timeframes once you left the fashion theater lobby."

He pointed to the coconut shell. "Perhaps you doubled back to the convention center, entered the fashion theater, encountered Mr. Posnick, and *finished your final conversation with him...*"

Arms akimbo, Mariel's glare showed her displeasure. But she kept her yap shut and resisted giving him the satisfaction of a response to his last-ditch fishing expedition.

Mo put the container holding the coconut shell back inside the evidence bag. He slid the notebook and pencil inside his jacket pocket and stood.

He said, "I appreciate your time, Ms. Levine. Those are all my questions for today, but I might have more to ask, so don't make any plans to go out of town."

Chapter Fourteen

Crammed between a needlepoint store and a nail salon, The Fish Shanty on Ocean Drive in Lauderdale-by-the-Sea is a locals' hole-in-the-wall that is easy to miss. Modestly decorated with colorful seashells and starfish hung on a series of fishnet-covered walls, the cozy eatery housed only a dozen wooden tables and ladderback chairs.

While it doesn't have a full bar, the restaurant is famous for its huge beer and wine selection. The house specialty is fresh grouper sautéed in white wine and shallots, served with zucchini fritters, oven-roasted red potatoes, and the tartest, tastiest key lime pie on the planet for dessert. I always peruse the extensive, four-page menu featuring many yummy-sounding dishes. But I am a true creature of habit, and in all the years I've eaten at The Fish Shanty, I've never ordered anything other than the house special.

The server took our orders, and then Mom asked, "So, what's your take on the interrogation?"

I pointed to the fishnet-covered walls. "Mo went on a fishing trip and came home empty-handed. He threw out some tempting bait, but Mariel refused to bite. Other than the coconut shell that Mariel admitted was hers, Mo got the big hole from the bagel from her. Four witnesses can corroborate that she left the fashion theater in possession of the coconut, threw it away into a trash container in the theater lobby, and exited the theater complex not in possession of the coconut."

Mom held up three fingers. "Three witnesses, not four."

I looked at her oddly. "Which one of the four didn't see Mariel toss the coconut?'

Mom tapped an index finger into her cleavage. "Me."

"You? Why were you wandering around? We agreed you'd wait in the same spot in the lobby where we stood earlier."

"I didn't wander around, but I did visit the ladies' room."

"Okay. So?"

Mom pursed her lips. "So, I didn't *personally* witness Mariel *physically* deposit the coconut into the lobby trash container."

"Well, she was holding it before you went into the restroom, right?"

Mom nodded.

"And she wasn't holding it when you returned to the group, right?"

Mom nodded again.

"And none of the other three were holding the coconut when you returned from the restroom, right?"

"Correct."

"And there was no reason for Mariel to hand the coconut to one of the others to toss in the trash container, right?"

"No reason."

I rolled my eyes. "So, unless the coconut fairy swooped down and snatched it out of Mariel's hands sometime between you entering the ladies' room and your return to the group, it is a pretty safe bet that Mariel is who threw the coconut into the theater lobby trash can while you were in the ladies' room."

Mom grinned and gave me the middle finger salute. "Even as a little kid, you always were a wiseass...a personality trait, by the way, you inherited genetically from your *father's side of the family*. Your Uncle Barry specifically comes to mind."

You'll get no argument from me.

I blew Mom a kiss and bowed from the waist. "Just part of my charm, but be that as it may, Mariel might not be able to prove she went home and stayed home, but Mo can't prove she didn't. All Mo has is a bucket full of insinuations. He has nothing, other than the coconut she admitted was hers, to *physically tie Mariel* to the crime scene. If he did, then she'd be wearing an orange jumpsuit and be a guest of the Graybar hotel tonight."

Mom batted her eyelids. "Speaking of Mo..."

I blushed from my neck to my scalp. "What about him?"

Mom gave me the stink eye. "That's what I'm trying to find out. So...?"

I shrugged. "I dunno."

Mom rolled her eyes. "Come on, Hol. Cut out the crap. Either he still curls your toes, or he doesn't."

I stared down at my plate and pushed a forkful of zucchini fritters around for something to do with my hands. "It's complicated."

Mom laughed out loud. "No kidding."

I whined like a cranky toddler. "*Mo...ther, you're not helping.*"

"Sure, I am. I'm helping *you think.*"

I clucked my tongue. "I wasn't aware I needed any help thinking."

"Well, apparently, you do. You and this man share a history. The question is, do you want to share a future with him?"

I sighed. "Until forty-eight hours ago, I hadn't given Moisés Lehrman a thought in years. But I'd be lying if I said a bolt of electric current didn't sizzle through my body when he walked into the storage room."

Mom pursed her lips. "So, was an electric current your body's response to the shock of unexpectedly seeing him, or does he still curl your toes?"

"Maybe a little bit of both."

"So now?"

"I dunno if there is any now to it."

"Why?"

"Geography. My life is in LA, and his life is in Miami."

Mom rolled her eyes. "People do move..."

I sighed. "This relationship is destined to fail if the price one of us pays is to sacrifice the life they've worked hard to build. If resentment is always just below the surface, eventually, the relationship is doomed to end."

Mom tsked. "It's not a sacrifice if the other person is the most important one in your life. And if the other person is, they made the change willingly."

I shook my head. "Even if the scenario were all true, the last thing my love life needs is *another cop*. The first one didn't work out so well." I grinned. "For some inexplicable reason, even when you solve their cases for them, they still get cranky if you stick your nose in their business and tell them how to do their job."

"Putting your investigative antics aside, let's not forget Mo's competition."

I snapped, "It isn't a contest."

Mom jutted her jaw. "Isn't it? Two men are competing to win the hand of the same woman. It sure sounds like one to me."

I blew the air out of my cheeks. "Geez, you make it sound as if I'm first prize at the county fair. And for the record, neither of them knows about the other one, and I want to keep it that way. So, there is no contest between them."

Mom widened her eyes. "Kiddo, you are playing with fire. One way or another, they *will* find out, and if you're not careful, you'll end up losing them both. But the question remains. *How about Buddy*? Since Miguel is out of the picture, it seemed as if you and Buddy were getting serious."

I nodded. "Yes, that's true. We are...er...were."

Mom raised her eyebrows. "Or, the question is if there *was no Buddy*, how does it change things between you and Mo?"

"But there is a Buddy *and* a Mo."

"And now?"

"And now I have to scratch the itch, or it'll drive me insane."

Mom gave me the stink eye. "And you think that *one evening* together with him will give you the answers one way or another?"

"I hope so. Since I'll be going home in a few days, that's as good as it can get. Besides, nothing is better than putting distance between two people to get their relationship into its proper perspective."

Mom squared her shoulders. "Mo Lehrman is a fine man who cares deeply for you. Don't toy with his emotions and hurt him by starting something you either can't or choose not to see through. Remember, regret is the worst human emotion because it is the one we can usually do nothing about."

I grinned. "You sound like Nana."

Mom smiled at the memory. "Who better to emulate?"

Mom cleared her throat. "Speaking of Nana, do you have time to go out and see her this trip? You've never been to the cemetery since the day of her funeral...S-she's been gone a long time, Hol."

My heart ached for my mother as her voice caught.

I could not imagine life *without my mother*.

Mom reached across the table and squeezed my hand. "Isn't it about time you visited her? I bet she'd love you to. We'll go together. What do you say?"

I held my hands out as if warding off a blow. "I'm sorry, but no. It's not as if I don't want to visit her. But I can't bring myself to stand at her grave and read her name and *date of death* chiseled into the marker."

My eyes filled. "It finalizes her death and the reality that she is gone *forever*. I prefer to do what I always do. I pretend she's on a Caribbean cruise with Katie Moskowitz. She's sightseeing, playing canasta, eating two decadent desserts after dinner, dancing with the purser, flirting with the ship's captain, and having a grand time. *That* is the way I choose to picture Nana forever."

I looked Mom in the eye. "It might be childish, or unrealistic, or foolish, but if I didn't play that mind game, I couldn't bear to come to Miami."

Chapter Fifteen

The Next Morning

The Yentas were all ears as I related the details of Mariel Levine's interrogation.

Joan clucked her tongue. "So, in your opinion, despite *Mariel's coconut* being the *murder weapon* and a fabric swatch of *her blouse* attached to it, she is out of the woods as a suspect?"

I nodded. "Yeah. Anyone could have seen Mariel throw the coconut into the lobby trash container and wait around until the place cleared out and retrieve it."

Sonia stroked her chin. "And three witnesses watched her throw the coconut into the lobby trash container, and four observed her exiting the building without the coconut."

I said, "There were more witnesses."

Joan looked at me oddly and counted the names on her fingertips. "Four. Your mother. Avril Wilts. Avril's two bosses."

I pointed to the security cameras mounted in each corner of the ceiling of the coffee shop. "Security cameras are stationed in the fashion theater and the lobby."

Sonia said, "If security cameras are backstage and in the storage room, the murder was filmed."

I shook my head. "Mo would have viewed the film by now and arrested the killer. Since no one was arrested based on any security film identifications, either no security cameras were in the storage room, or the killer wore a mask or faced away from the camera."

Joan wrinkled her nose. "Sorry, Holly, but Mariel isn't off the hook. Let's say the security cameras in the lobby prove she threw the coconut away. Say she exited the building without it. It doesn't prove she's innocent. She could have circled back, retrieved the coconut, lured Simon to the storage room, and done the deed."

Sonia shook her head. "That's not a plausible scenario. First of all, the lobby security camera would have filmed her in the act. But even if she managed to retrieve the coconut undetected and meet up with Simon, what excuse would she use to lure him into the storage room? None that I can think of. Simon was an obnoxious bully, but he wasn't stupid, and he would have refused to go with her."

I said, "While Mariel can prove she disposed of the coconut before she left the theater building, she can't prove she got home at the time she claimed and never left, but Mo can't prove otherwise."

Hope scratched the crown of her head. "Okay, if we eliminate Mariel as a suspect, it leaves Avril Wilts, her bosses, the twins, and Walter Seiden..."

Joan sighed. "And half the vendors at the trade show who probably had a beef with Simon Posnick at one time or another."

I bit my lower lip. "Without a confession, it's impossible to pin the murder on one of them until the coroner completes the autopsy. No suspects can be eliminated until the height, weight, and gender of the killer, which of their hands held the murder weapon when they impaled the jagged edge into Simon's head, and the angle of the thrust of the coconut as it penetrated the back of his skull are all determined."

Joan lobbed one of her well-practiced zingers. "*And of course, the Dade County Coroner will gladly hand over the autopsy results to you if you ask sweetly.*"

I grinned. "It's not what you know but who you know who gets you where you want to go. Jasmine Jones, the assistant coroner assigned to the Posnick case, went through medical school with Dr. Sophie Cutler, my lifelong friend."

I snapped my fingers. "Piece of cake."

Chapter Sixteen

S*even forty-five p.m. that evening*

It was a balmy seventy-five degrees. A slight northern breeze tickled your fancy while keeping the humidity manageable. Mo and I sat next to one another, facing the aquamarine Atlantic at a cozy table for two on the patio of Adam Fong's China Mist Café. The sun dipped below the horizon, painting the sky with a kaleidoscope of tropical colors as the orb was swallowed into oblivion.

I bit my lip not to laugh as I watched the skinny whisp of a waiter, pushing eighty if he was a day, struggle to balance the huge stainless-steel tray loaded with eight plates of steaming hot dishes on his narrow shoulder. Once he set all the plates on the table, there wasn't a square inch of free space.

I fanned all the plates. "Are we expecting others to join us, or haven't you eaten in several days?"

Mo grinned. "Neither. This is the way you order at a grazing-style restaurant."

I puckered my lips. "Grazing? The same way as a herd of cattle eats? I ought to be insulted."

He rolled his eyes. "No. *Grazing is the term for nibbling a variety of appetizers*." He picked up his chopsticks and pointed to the feast of food in front of us. "A smorgasbord for two. It's simple. Look at the items on each dish. Pick one that looks interesting. Pluck it with your chopsticks, and eat it."

To demonstrate, Mo leaned over the table, deftly plucked a Krab Rangoon Wonton off the plate with the tips of his chopsticks, and popped it into his mouth. I admired his chopstick prowess. Unlike

Miguel Martinez, my LAPD ex-beau, who never got the hang of it, no matter how many times I taught him, Moisés Lehrman knew his way around a set of chopsticks.

I pointed my chopsticks at the plateful of Krab Rangoon Wonton. "How did you know I've been dying for Chinese food?"

He wiggled his brows. "I could say I'm clairvoyant and impress you with my powers of prediction, but the truth is I interviewed your mother this morning at Laurie's, and she mentioned it."

"We were busy all day, and I never had a chance to speak to my mother. How did her interview go?"

Mo's back stiffened. "Come on, Hol, you know better. I can't comment on an active investigation."

I rolled my eyes. "It's not as if you questioned a stranger. You interviewed *my mother*. You do realize I'll get the lowdown from her anyway, don't you? This way, you can give me your take on her answers to your questions."

He made a sour face.

I shrugged. "Fine. Suit yourself. I'll be at Laurie's tomorrow afternoon for a meeting with Mariel."

In an attempt to change the subject to one less dicey, Mo snapped his fingers and said, "By the way, I meant to congratulate you on buying Mermaid Swimwear. Quite an achievement." He grinned. "I started to say something in the storage room, but it seemed inappropriate to be congratulatory with a bloody corpse lying only a few feet away."

I laughed. "I'd ask how you found out, but since the telephone, telegraph, tell Mike Schlivnik, who tells it to Abe Lehrman, so, obviously, it was my father."

Mo smiled. "No wonder the daddios are BFFs. They were the two biggest Yentas in the apparel industry."

No kidding.

"Harriet Kaplan, who took over my territory when I moved back to LA, replaced Dad when he retired. Now that Abe had turned the business over to your sisters, Harriet called Miriam for a market appointment. But Miriam said she and your sisters weren't coming to the trade show and would work with Harriet in the mart the following week. I'm disappointed. I was looking forward to seeing Miriam, Esther, and Ruth."

Mo nodded. "The girls are not the social butterflies our dad is. They don't like all the hoopla of a trade show. They prefer to see lines, especially the important ones like yours, in a quieter setting. That way, they can concentrate on the product with no noise or interruptions."

I counted the sisters on my fingers. "Miriam is the CEO and in charge of fashion and buying. Esther is the CFO. Ruth is in charge of operations. What does Deborah do?"

Mo tapped his chest. "Like her older brother, the baby of the family chose a different route. Deborah is in her first year of medical school at the University of Miami."

"Wow. All five Lehrman children have made their parents proud."

My stomach rumbled a reminder that the tuna on rye I gulped down between customer appointments was a distant memory. "Let's dig in while the food is hot." I scrunched my nose. "Chinese food is not great ice cold."

I snagged a Szechuan potsticker and moaned with delight. "This is insanely delicious. I'd be perfectly happy just eating these and nothing else."

Mo nodded. "You could, but you'd miss the entire point of eating at a grazing restaurant." He speared a chicken dumpling and bit it in half. He hovered the chopsticks with the other half of the dumpling between them next to my lips. "Taste this. It's sensational."

He slid the dumpling into my mouth. I chewed languidly, and my taste buds exploded from the tangy sauce. I lolled my head back with pleasure. "Mmm. Heavenly."

I picked a vegetable spring roll off the plate and dipped it into some soy sauce. I bit into it and fed the other half to Mo.

I used my baby finger to dab a smear of soy sauce off his chin.

He licked the sauce off my finger, and the world tilted.

His eyes never left mine as he fed me a piece of barbequed chicken on a skewer.

He curled his right leg around my left one.

My pulse pounded in my ears as he pulled me closer until our faces were only inches apart.

I couldn't focus as he parted my lips with his chopsticks to feed me a Krab Rangoon Wonton.

The spicy Szechuan potstickers weren't to blame for my every nerve being on fire.

This was too erotic to call a meal.

An experience this sensual wasn't eating.

This was food sex.

We fed one another the remaining items slowly, taking great pleasure in watching one another chew each bite.

What the hell was I doing?

I had no idea.

But whatever it was, I was helpless to stop the undercurrent of urgency that left us both breathless.

Chapter Seventeen

The valet drove Mo's cherry red classic muscle car convertible to the restaurant entrance. Mo opened the passenger door, and I slid into the well-worn bucket seat. Despite all the years of being apart, my body still responded to the familiarity of the leather, like coming home to a favorite easy chair.

Mo tipped the valet and scooted into the driver's seat. He unhooked a metal clip on each side of the canvas top. Next, he pressed a button on the dashboard, and the convertible top motor whirred to life as the canvas folded into the well behind the back seats.

I tilted my head back and drank in the beauty of millions of twinkling stars dangling from the inky black, clear sky.

He asked, "Do you still drive your mother's pink convertible?"

I smiled. "Yep. Thanks to my mechanic, who keeps her in tip-top shape, she still runs smooth as silk."

Mo stroked the tufted dashboard like he would a lover's cheek. "This baby has two hundred and twenty-five thousand miles on her, but I can't imagine driving anything else. My dad and I do most of the upkeep. Thank goodness parts are still available for classic cars like this."

I asked, "Do you still sail your Venture?"

"No. I sold it a few years ago."

My jaw dropped. "*You stopped sailing?* Really? I can't imagine it."

He shook his head. "No. Once a sailor, always a sailor. Sailing is as much a part of my life as breathing. I could no more stop sailing than stop inhaling and exhaling. One of Dad's dress suppliers owned a forty-four-foot Universal in mint condition. The poor guy suffered a stroke and was unable to sail anymore. He offered it to Dad for next to nothing. I sold the Venture, and we pooled our money and bought the Universal together. I sail her more than Dad, but since he's retired, he'll take her out more often. You still sail. I heard you bought a thirty-foot Adventura rigged for single sailing, right?"

Hmm...First, my business, now my boat. For someone out of my life, he certainly knew an awful lot about it. An odd combination of thrill and annoyance fought for control of my heart.

I nodded. "I did, but once I started traveling more frequently, I hardly ever took the boat out. The high upkeep for something I rarely used didn't make sense, so I sold the sailboat and bought a houseboat. I live on it in Marina del Rey with my standard poodle Sigmund Freud."

He grinned. "Sigmund Freud? As in the shrink?"

Is there another one?

"Yep. I tell Siggie everything. He's my four-legged shrink."

Mo raised his eyebrows.

"Hey, don't knock it. Siggie is an excellent listener. He never interrupts, never tells me my hour is up just as I get to the heart of a problem, and doesn't charge a hundred and fifty bucks an hour."

Mo punched a button on the radio, and a surf group from the sixties sang in perfect harmony. We grinned at one another and burst into an off-key sing-along.

Mo and I shared many interests. Rock n' roll oldies, smooth jazz, convertible cars, sailing, mushroom and onion pizza, Chinese food, and Rocky Road ice cream topped the list.

Mo asked, "Did you leave any room for dessert? An Uncle Izzy's Ice Cream Emporium is only a few blocks from your hotel. Izzy's Rocky Road is hands-down the best in the city, and they are the only ones who still serve their ice cream in a sugar cone."

Was he kidding? After the meal we just shared?

I patted my tummy. "Sorry, I'm stuffed."

Three blocks from my hotel, he glanced at the clock on the dashboard.

Nine o'clock.

A melancholy tone of longing tempered his deep voice. "It's still early..."

He didn't want the evening to end, and honestly, neither did I.

He apologized. "I would suggest a nightcap, but technically, I'm on duty."

He snapped his fingers. "How about a walk on the beach? It's been a long time since we've seen one another. We've got a lot to catch up on."

I smiled. "Sounds perfect."

I fished the room key out of my messenger bag as he pulled into the hotel entrance. "I'll show the valet my room key so you won't pay for parking. They charge an arm and a leg for non-guests."

He said, "No worries. I've got something even better."

He reached behind him for an MBPD ID laminated placard for the dashboard.

We made a quick trip up to my room so I could exchange my messenger bag for a fanny pack and heels for sandals. Ten minutes later, we strolled companionly along the deserted shoreline barefoot with our pant legs rolled up to our knees.

It was low tide, and the glassy ocean tickling our toes was the tepid temperature of two-hour-old bath water. A July "Buck Moon," the brightest supermoon, lit up the inky sky. The stars diamond-danced their reflections onto the placid water, gently lapping the shore.

Mo motioned to the hotel. "Whoever bought the Caribe Royale spent a bucket of bucks to restore it to its heyday in the twenties and added a memorable feature. Have you seen the roof?"

I narrowed my eyes. "What's so special about *a roof*?"

"It's an incredible rooftop *garden* with every imaginable type of tropical plants—including banana trees and coconut palms, as well as several well-placed waterfalls. I've never seen anything like it. It's like being in a rainforest. Chairs and tables in a tropical décor are set up throughout the garden for guests to relax. Putting a lush garden on the roof was a genius idea."

"Wow. It sounds spectacular. I'll have to check it out."

Mo said, "And the Art Deco lobby is something else. It is an authentic throwback to the twenties. They advertise that every room has a panoramic view. If your room is an example of the rest, I might never leave. A hotel room with a panoramic view like yours is rare."

I nodded. "Some of the girls have a city view. Mine has a spectacular ocean view. The sunrises are magnificent."

He wiggled his brows. "Gee, I'd love to see a sunrise from your room."

I laughed. "Make a reservation, request my room number, and ta-da!"

He asked, "Have you stayed at the hotel before, or is this your first time?"

"First time. I stayed with my parents during the trade shows while my dad was still the sales rep. That way, we spent more time together, and Dad and I strategized during the drives back and forth. The other times I come to visit, I always stay with my parents."

"Do you come to Miami often?"

"Since my folks are older, I come down as often as possible. I always try to include a stopover in Miami after a New York market or if I'm going to an account in the Southern region."

"So, you're in Miami a few times a year, and yet you've never called me. How come?"

"There was no point in starting something I couldn't finish."

He flinched, but mercifully changed the conversation's direction. "It must be quite odd for you to be at a Miami trade show, and neither of our dads is at the convention center."

I nodded. "That's the understatement of the year. It has taken some time and a major effort for me to get used to my father's retirement. Intellectually, I understand Dad wanted to retire and enjoy himself. But emotionally, it's a different story. I'd never spent a day in the apparel business without my father." I laughed. "What goes around comes around. Now I understand the feeling of loss Dad went through when I resigned from our sales organization and moved back to LA." My eyes filled. "A part of me is missing, and there's a hollow place in my heart I'll never be able to fill."

My pulse raced as Mo entwined his fingers in mine and gently squeezed. "Have you spoken to him this trip? It's hard to imagine him not calling to see how things were running without him."

I shook my head. "Monte Carlo is six hours ahead of Miami. It's either too early or too late to call. My parents speak to one another every other day, so I'm sure he's up to speed on the market."

"Does he know about the murder?"

"No. I asked my mother not to say anything."

"So, he has no idea you and I are...sort of reunited?"

I burst out laughing. "Are you kidding? Not a chance...unless you told your mother and she mentioned it to Abe. Give my father the smallest sniff of a reunion, and trust me, the daddios would be on the next flight home to plan our engagement party."

Mo brushed away a lock of hair that a gust of wind had blown into my eyes. We were so close that I grew heady from the citrusy scent of his cologne. His voice was deep and reedy. "And how is that bad? You can't deny that there is something still between us."

I could, but I'd be lying...

My heart and better judgment were locked in mortal combat. With my nerves buzzing like a runaway electric current, I had to cool off or run the risk of doing something I'd later regret. I ran to the water's edge and waded in up to my knees. Mo followed me in and got in front of me. I banged my arms on the surface and splashed him, getting him soaking wet. He retaliated by shoveling two huge handfuls of water all over the front of my blouse. I tried to run back to the beach, but he caught me by the belt loop. He scooped a handful of water up and poured it down my pants.

I wriggled out of his clutches and ran to shore. I danced an awkward imitation of the hokey-pokey as something slimy slithered down my leg. Mo tackled me from behind, but as I went down, I hooked my ankle around his and tripped him. Laughing like a couple of crazy loons, we rolled around locked together in the sand until we were coated from head to toe.

We stilled, and as we lay entwined in one another's arms, he kissed me like I'd never been kissed before.

Chapter Eighteen

We rinsed off the outer layers of sand at the shower next to the beach cabanas. I patted Mo's tush, and the sand still inside his pants shifted, and it looked like he had a load. "You'll ruin the car's leather seats if the insides of your clothes are full of sand."

He shrugged. "Loan me a few towels, and I'll lay them on the driver's seat."

I shook my head. "Still no good. You'll never get all the sand out of the interior. Once the car sits in the hot sun, it'll smell worse than a dirty aquarium after the wet sand dries. And no matter how many times you clean the car, you'll never get rid of the smell. The only thing to do is come up to my room and shower. I'll call the hotel's twenty-four-hour laundry service and ask for an emergency pick-up. It'll cost a fortune, but your clothes will be clean to go home in."

He waved his hand. "I'm a cop. I keep an emergency change of clothes stashed in the trunk of my car."

"That's a much better option. Let me into my room. Then take the key and get your bag. By the time you come back up, I'll be out of the shower, and you can take your turn."

I couldn't stand the sand scratching and chafing every crevice when I moved. I almost shoved Mo out the door and raced into the bathroom. I tore my clothes off and tossed them into a laundry bag. I turned the hot water to full blast and scrubbed myself raw from head to toe. Sand was in every orifice of my body—from up my ass crack to inside my vagina, to my nostrils, to the openings of my ears. It took three rounds of shampooing to get the beachful of sand out of my hair. When I finished, a layer of sand coated the bottom of the tub up to my ankles. I drained the sand out and doubted that I had left any hot water for Mo.

I slipped into a plush terry bathrobe and wrapped a towel around my wet hair. I walked out of the steamy bathroom to the closet. As I stepped into my slippers, the key turned, and Mo opened the door. He dropped his getaway bag on the floor and drank in every part of me with hungry eyes.

I deadpanned, "There's a possibility that I didn't leave you any hot water..."

He grinned wolfishly. "We should have showered together to conserve it."

Hopefully, a cold shower would cool the evening down to a reasonable temperature for both of us.

I shooed him into the bathroom. The moment he closed the door, the room temperature dropped fifty degrees, and a blast of icy cold air chilled me to the bone. I pulled my bathrobe tighter as two swirls of twin tornadoes emitting freezing air spun counterclockwise. They whirred on either side of me and morphed into my two favorite apparitions.

Justine LaValle took a look at Marie's stone-faced expression and sensed a storm was brewing. Buddy's baby girl wisely hid behind her mother.

Marie LaValle stood arms akimbo. Her toe tapped with impatience, and daggers of fury sparked in her dark eyes. She pinched her cheeks in tight as if she had sucked on a sour lemon. Icicles covered my face as she shot the words out of her puckered lips like a machine gun. "Jest what in the Sam Damn Hill are you doin', girlie, cavortin' like some floozy with ano*ther man* when your hand is already promised to mah Cajun boy? We had this same conversation not seventy-two hours ago, and yet here we are again. Ah cain't leave you alone for a minute without your eye wandering." She pointed to the closed bathroom door. "And now, a *naked man is* in your shower who most certainly *ain't* mah Buddy!

If ya'll know what's good for ya, ya'll best make the man put on some clothes and git decent. Then show the interloper the way out and lock the damned door."

I lasered her with my finely-honed death ray glare, normally reserved for pain in the patootie buyers. "I'm sick of you continuously sticking your nose into my business and ordering me around as if you're in charge of my life. For your information, Buddy *still* wears his *wedding ring*. Not a day passes that he doesn't say, '*Gee, if only Marie could see me now*.' Have you ever been to his house?" I pointed to Marie and Justine in a *j'accuse* style. "The place is a shrine to your memories. Pictures of you and Justine hang as a memorial on every single wall. Buddy moved across the country to start over, but he brought you two along. You might be ready for him to move on, but clearly, he isn't and may *never* be. I'm not the one to haunt into action. Your Cajun boy is."

I jabbed my index finger under her nose to emphasize my point, and it froze. "Lemme tell you something, Miss High and Mighty. If your Cajun boy requires pushing and prodding, moving on isn't right for him. And I'll be damned if I'm going to beg. I won't deny I have feelings for him. I do. But I can't...no, I'm *not willing* to compete with the ghosts of his dead wife and daughter. It's a contest I'd never win, so forget it. I refuse to wait for the rest of my life for Buddy to get over you and Justine. Maybe he's incapable or doesn't want to move on, *but I do*." Marie's jaw dropped as I growled a lot louder than I meant to. "So, do us all a favor and move on to the next place you're supposed to go and get the *hell out of my life*!"

The bathroom door opened, and the two ghosts vanished into thin air as Mo stepped out with only a towel draped around his narrow hips. His broad shoulders picture-framed tightly curled tufts of dark brown chest hair. Beads of water glistened like pearls on the wet strands of his tousled, wavy brown hair. Oh. My. Goddess.

He looked at me oddly. "I could have sworn I heard voices."

I shrugged.

He glanced at the dark television.

"Were you talking to someone?"

My mind drew a blank.

Zip. Zero. Nada. Nothing.

My cell phone rang.

The Goddess threw me a life preserver.

Caller ID said, *Buddy*.

Okay, not a life preserver.

A noose to hang myself with.

I stared at the blinking phone screen, willing it to stop.

One ring. Two rings. Three rings. Four rings.

So much for my powers of persuasion.

Mo asked, "Are you going to answer it or just let it go to voicemail? Is it a wrong number? Or someone you don't want to talk to right now?"

You have no idea...

I waved Mo off and pressed the talk button. "Hello, Buddy. How are you? Mmm-hmm. Yeah, I'm sorry. Yes, you're right. It's been a couple of days. We've been packed from open to close and entertained retailers in the evenings. With the time change, if I were free, it was either too late or too early to call you."

I turned my back on Mo for a modicum of privacy.

"Yes, it is late. No, I wasn't asleep, but now's not a good time for me to talk. I'm actually with someone. No, not a buyer. An old friend. It's been a few years since the last time we saw one another, and we're catching up."

Fingers of guilt wrapped themselves around my heartstrings and tied them into knots so tight they almost strangled my poor ticker. I hated myself for lying. Buddy deserved better, but he wasn't prepared for the truth, and honestly, neither was I.

"The market will be winding down in a day or two, so I will have some free time to call you in then. Okay? Great. Yeah, I miss you too, honey...Bye."

I forced myself to face Mo.

He arched a brow. "My competition, I presume?"

Was my love life a topic of conversation between Mo and my mother while he interrogated her?

I snapped, "This isn't a contest, so there is no competition."

His voice rasped with desire. "*I'll make absolutely sure of that.*"

My eyes widened as he closed the distance between us.

He left no space between our bodies.

My breath caught as he loosened my bathrobe tie.

My skin was on fire as his fingertips caressed my shoulders.

> My pulse spiked as he brushed his lips across the small of my neck.
>
> I gasped as his lips feathered my neck with soft kisses.
>
> My heart hammered as his lips teased my cleavage.

My knees went wobbly as the robe slipped away.

And then the world bent sideways.

Chapter Nineteen

The night before had been pure magic, but dawn brought more questions than answers. One thing was certain: overnight, my life became complicated in ways I never imagined possible.

I was uncharacteristically twenty minutes late the next morning as I dragged my weary bones into the Brews & Bagels and headed to the back table.

Joan looked over the rims of her eyeglasses and tossed out one of her sharp-as-a-steak-knife zingers. "Well, look who decided to *finally* grace us with her presence this glorious morning." She lifted her wrist, a watch strapped to it, to illustrate her point. "You arrived just in the nick of time. Another minute and we were ready to send out a search party."

I eased my tush into a chair. "And a glorious good morning to you, too, Joanie."

Sonia handed me a steaming hot cup of coffee. I toasted Joan and glugged an industrial-sized, restorative slurp.

Queenie gave me the once-over and smirked. "Those dark smudges under your eyes are rather sexy. Add them to your makeup routine for a mysterious look."

My response was the middle finger salute.

She ignored me. "Late night or early morning?"

I smiled sheepishly. "Maybe a little of both."

Joan smirked. "Nothing like burning the candle at both ends to do you in the next day."

Sonia studied me with a level of curiosity normally afforded to a newly-discovered species. "You look as if a bus ran over you. Yet, there's something gloriously different about you, but I can't quite put my finger on it."

Hope's eyes gleamed with recognition. "You're right. Something is definitely different. She's got an aura, a glow."

Hope queried the table. "It's not just me, right, girls?"

Joan looked me up and down. "Yep, she's got it, all right. She's positively glowing bright enough to light up the city."

I blushed from my neck to my hairline.

Hope wiggled her eyebrows and giggled like a naughty schoolgirl. "And there's *only one way you get a glow that bright.*"

Joan shoved two fingers between her lips and let go a wolf whistle loud enough to turn every head in the place toward our table. "Oh yeah. There is only *one way* to get it, girls. Yes, indeed, she most certainly did *get it*. Woo-hoo!"

I opened my mouth to deny their insinuation, but the words died in my throat. Who was I kidding? You'd have to be blind not to see it. The truth was written all over my face.

It was a relief to get to our booth. We worked nonstop until three o'clock. There was no time for my mind to stray into uncomfortable territory...or any opportunity to call Buddy.

I scheduled a four o'clock meeting with Mariel Levine at Laurie's executive office to finalize the ad styles for our statewide billboard campaign. Lauren packed the presentation into a canvas garment bag. I made a potty stop and grabbed a tuna sandwich on the run.

A wet blanket of humidity covered me as I went out the exit on the A1A side of the convention center to get into the taxi queue. I glanced at my watch. Three-thirty on the nose. No queue. No cabs. Huh? I panicked. If a cab didn't come by soon, I'd have to ask my mother to pick me up.

Fortunately, I remembered Tyrell. I fished his business card out of the bottom of my messenger bag. I prayed he wasn't on the other side of the city and made the call. I'd no sooner pressed the end button than Tyrell pulled up to the curb. Either his business was incredibly slow, or he lived in his cab. Thank the Goddess, Tyrell turned the AC up to the blizzard level as I scooted into the back seat. He made the OK sign as I gave him the destination. He hooked a U-turn and blasted out of the parking lot onto another traffic-jammed A1A going northbound. This time, I was prepared. I tightened my seatbelt, closed my eyes, and whispered a prayer. One thing was sure: I'd be on time for the meeting...if I lived through the ride. Tyrell dropped me off with five minutes to spare.

The receptionist announced me and slid a visitor's badge across the counter. A few minutes later, my mother came up to the reception area and escorted me to the executive suite.

As we approached Mariel's office, Mom gave me the once-over and smirked. "Those dark smudges under your eyes are quite attractive...actually, downright sexy. Late night or early morning?"

Do Queenie and my mother share a hotline?

I rewarded my mother with the same middle finger salute I gave Queenie.

Chapter Twenty

I hung the samples on the grid and laid the fabric swatches and line list on the conference table between Mom and her boss.

Mariel said, "The billboards will roll out by region. The earliest rollout will go live on October 1st and will cover the southern counties. The second rollout will go live on November 1st and will cover the mid-state counties. The third rollout will go live on January 1st and will cover the northern and panhandle counties."

I noted the information in Laurie's account folder, then the three of us rearranged the samples by rollout delivery. Mom marked a line list with the styles and colors they selected, and the rollout delivery dates. She went into her office to put the orders into their open-to-buy computer system and print copies for us.

I asked, "Are we shipping your orders bulk or in pre-packs by store?"

Mariel said, "Pre-packs. You'll get bulk orders now, so you can go into production. You will receive the distributions for the prepacks a month before each delivery start date. Each one will have our standard fourteen-day ship window, with start and cancel dates. The delivery start dates are pegged to the billboards. You'll receive the distributions a month before the billboard rollouts go live. This will give you sufficient time to ship and us to receive the goods before the billboards are up."

I nodded. "Yes, that'll work. I'll fax the bulk orders to our production department tonight from the hotel business center. When will you be writing the non-ad orders?"

"I still have a few lines to see before we do our final style out next week. Your orders will be in your hands two weeks from now."

I said, "If you want October 30th deliveries for your fashion stores, I'll need the orders for those stores before I go back to Los Angeles. Two weeks from now for the rest of the orders is fine. We will still be quoting November 30th cancel dates."

Mariel said, "I'll work with Natalie on..."

Mom opened the passway between the two offices. "Excuse me, ladies. I hate to interrupt you, but the receptionist called and said that Detective Lehrman is in the lobby to see Mariel. What do you want me to say?"

Mariel clucked her tongue. "Tell Alicia to tell him that I'm in a meeting. He can either wait until we're finished or schedule a time for tomorrow."

"Okay."

Two minutes later, Mom stuck her head through the passway. She was as white as a sheet. "The detective said, and I quote: 'Tell Ms. Levine her meeting is over.'"

Before Mariel responded, Mo marched purposefully through Mariel's office door without knocking. He addressed me as if I were a stranger. "This is official police business. Please leave and close the door behind you."

I followed the order and stepped into Mom's office. A passageway connects Mom's small office and Mariel's large one with a split door. If someone sat at Mariel's conference table, they couldn't see the passageway.

Mom tapped a shushing finger to her lips and cracked the passageway door partially open. The two of us jockeyed our positions until we stacked one on top of the other like those Russian doll sets so as not to miss a word.

Chapter Twenty-One

Mariel stood, arms akimbo across her chest, and made no effort to disguise her annoyance. "You can't just march into my office, disrupt a meeting, and inform me it is over. Who the hell do you think you are? The Gestapo?"

Mo pulled a chair out and replied in a stone-cold tone that sent a shiver down my spine. "Sit down, Ms. Levine. This is how police interrogations work. The police ask questions, and you answer them *whenever and wherever* the police ask. We can do this here for your convenience, or at police headquarters if you prefer. It doesn't matter to me either way. But one way or the other, you're going to answer my questions *now*."

Mariel sat, but kept talking. "You interviewed me for over two hours the other day. What on Earth more do you want?"

Mo snarled. "Start by telling the truth."

Mariel reared back. "I told you the truth."

"No, you didn't. You said *three people witnessed* you disposing of the coconut into a trash container in the fashion theater lobby."

Mariel nodded. "Yes, I did."

Mo curled his upper lip. "Those three witnesses did not confirm your story."

Mariel pursed her lips. "It's not a *story*. That's what happened."

Mo shook his head. "Not according to them. They say you never threw the coconut away. And even if they witnessed you trashing it, it doesn't matter. Not if you retrieved it later."

Mariel spat the words out like watermelon seeds. "*They're lying*."

Mo shrugged. "They have no reason to lie."

I cupped my hand over Mom's ear and whispered. "Avril Wilts was under the impression she was getting an ad order from Laurie's. She was furious when she didn't. She found out about ours and told me, and I quote, '*That bitch. She'll get hers someday.*'"

Mom whispered back, "And she'd *lie to the police* and go so far as to get her bosses to commit perjury to get back at Mariel?"

I nodded. "Absolutely."

Mariel said, "Be that as it may, they are lying. Security cameras are in the fashion theater and the lobby. We waited a long time for the crowd to thin out before trying to leave the parking lot. Check the security film. I am sure I was picked up on it."

Mo's eyes turned darker than a moonless night. "I don't need you to tell me how to do my job. We reviewed every foot of film, both inside the theater and the lobby. You were picked up in one frame holding the coconut."

Mariel pointed to Mom's office. "Natalie will confirm I trashed the coconut."

Mo said, "Mrs. Schlivnik admitted she was in the ladies' room when you *allegedly* disposed of the coconut."

Mariel rolled her eyes. "For crying out loud, Detective, Natalie observed me holding the coconut before she went into the ladies' room. And she observed me empty-handed when she returned to our group. I didn't say abracadabra and poof, it disappeared. She told you she watched me leave the building *empty-handed*."

Mo narrowed his eyes. "How long has Mrs. Schlivnik worked for you?"

Mariel snapped, "What does her length of employment have to do with anything?"

Mo shrugged. "*Loyal employees have been known to cover for their bosses...*"

I growled, "The son of a bitch just questioned your integrity."

Mom patted my arm. "He's only trying to get a rise out of her, hoping she'll slip up. If he thought I lied for Mariel, he would have arrested me for perjury." She held out her wrists. "See. No handcuffs."

I whispered, "The reason he said it doesn't matter. The only thing that matters is that he did."

Mo said, "The fact is you lied, Ms. Levine."

Mariel threw her hands up in exasperation. "If I didn't throw it away, where exactly did I hide it?" She cupped her hands as if holding the coconut. "My purse wasn't large enough to hold it. I didn't carry a messenger bag or briefcase that night." She sneered. "Do you think I shoved the damned thing down my pants?"

The door to Mariel's office opened, and Mom gasped as two uniformed policemen stepped inside. Mo held out his hands and raised them palms faced up. "Stand up and put your hands behind your back nice and slow and easy. Mariel Levine, you are under arrest for the murder of Simon Posnick."

My mouth opened wide enough to catch flies.

Mariel's complexion paled white as a sheet, and she trembled from head to toe. She stumbled as she numbly complied with Mo's command. The older of the two uniforms kept his right hand on his service revolver as he took a card out of his shirt pocket with his left. He read Mariel her rights while the younger one unclipped a set of handcuffs from his utility belt. I flinched at the ominous click of the metal bracelets as they locked Mariel's wrists into place.

The two uniforms sandwiched Mariel between them as they marched her perp-walk style to the office door. I ran around to Mariel's door and blocked their passage. I ignored Mo's searing glare and laser-focused on Mariel's eyes widened by fear to the size of silver dollars.

I asked, "Mariel, do you have a lawyer?"

She shook her head. "Only the one who drew up our wills."

My knees knocked as loudly as an untuned car engine, but for Mariel's sake, I swallowed the quiver in my voice. "Okay. No problem. A criminal defense attorney will meet you at the police station."

I cupped my ear. "Listen carefully." I twisted my index finger and thumb together like an invisible key locking my lips. "*Do. Not. Utter. Another. Single. Word.*" I pointed to Mo. "No matter what he says or does, or the threats he makes, *do not react*. Keep your mouth shut until you meet with your attorney. Do you understand?"

Her eyes filled as she nodded yes. She mouthed thank you as I stepped aside and let the terrified prisoner and her police escort pass.

Chapter Twenty-Two

Word of Mariel's arrest raced through the convention center like wildfire. The following morning, I stopped at the newsstand in the hotel lobby and bought a copy of the *East Coast Apparel News.*

While Hope distributed the coffee, I laid the newspaper in the center of the table. The headline above the fold screamed, "***BIKINI BUYER BEHIND BARS***".

The mood at the Yenta table was subdued as I relayed the sordid details of Mariel's arrest. Mariel Levine was a powerful, popular, seasoned industry veteran who now stood accused of a vicious murder. Not one of my group believed she was guilty. Proving her innocence? Another story.

Saucy Joan slapped the table. "Thank the Goddess Mariel authorized all your purchase orders before they cuffed her and took her away."

Always practical, Sonia mused, "All kidding aside, who will handle the department while Mariel is in the slammer?"

I said, "I spoke to my mother early this morning. Mariel's arrest will not create any business disruption. Management gave my mother full authority to review product lines and to place orders. Mom and Mariel shopped the market together. She has all their notes, so she knows which styles and colors to buy."

Hope tapped her lower lip. "Sounds as if management has already passed judgment on Mariel."

Sonia shook her head. "Not necessarily. Management has no idea when *or if* Mariel will return. Their business must go on either way."

I mused, "Mariel better come back soon. My mother is a team player and willing to pitch in and do her part during a crisis, but this is *not* what she signed up for."

My cell phone rang. I glanced at the screen. Caller ID said Mo Lehrman. I let the call go to voicemail.

Hope asked, "Is anyone representing Mariel?"

I said, "Like my parents, the only attorney Mariel and her husband had was the one who drew up their wills. I called Ms. Markowitz. She is originally from Miami."

Sonia didn't have a lawyer when she was wrongly arrested for the murder of the office executive, Bunny Frank. I called my Uncle Barry, a personal injury attorney in Beverly Hills, for help, and he recommended Ms. Markowitz. "*If I ever found myself in trouble with the law, Rose Markowitz is the one attorney I'd ever call.*" The diminutive octogenarian criminal defense attorney extraordinaire saved Sonia Wilson's ass.

Sonia asked, "Is Ms. Markowitz licensed to practice law in Florida?'

"No, but Lois Lowenstein, Ms. M's niece, is. Ms. M. contacted Lois, and she took the case. She met Mariel at the police station."

Sonia asked, "You and Ms. Lowenstein met?"

I nodded. "Yes. My mother, Mariel's husband, and I met with her last night after she interviewed Mariel."

I grinned. "Lo-Lo, as Ms. M referred to her as, is a taller, younger version of her aunt. She has Ms. M's eyes, nose, a take-no-prisoners personality, and doesn't take crap from anyone or let her clients get pushed around."

My cell phone rang again.

Mo Lehrman.

I ignored the call.

Queenie pursed her lips. "It's a good thing that Mariel is well-represented. She needs all the help she can get. Detective Lehrman laid out one helluva strong case."

Analytical Sonia tapped an index finger on her lower lip. "It may seem like Mariel's goose is cooked. The detective might have had enough evidence to arrest her, but he had no smoking gun."

Hope's eyes bulged. "How can you say there's no smoking gun? *Mariel's* coconut with a fabric swatch from *her blouse* was attached to it and embedded into the base of Simon Posnick's skull. Even though she said she tossed the coconut into the trash, no one witnessed her doing it."

I shook my head. "On the contrary, Hope. *Three people* in the fashion theater lobby witnessed her tossing it away. They're lying now. I'm going to get in their faces and force them to tell the truth."

And the Yentas' response? A well-practiced, synchronized groan.

Joan rolled her eyes. "You may have set a new record for sticking your nose where it doesn't belong."

I pointed a teaspoon at each of my colleagues. "Mariel Levine is no more a murderer than any of you. Mo Lehrman rushed to close a case with weak circumstantial evidence that any good lawyer could easily dispute, and arrested the wrong person. So, the real killer is still at large. And no one in the industry is safe until the monster is captured. Simon Posnick was no choir boy, but he didn't deserve to be murdered." I jutted my chin. "Mariel Levine stood up for me. Now it's my turn to stand up for her. Either help me figure this out or not, but either way, I'm not going to let Mariel down."

Queenie silently surveyed the girls around the table and sighed. "Okay, Hol. You win. We're in. Are there any other viable suspects?"

"Walter Seiden. He didn't do the happy dance at Simon's arrival at the fashion show. If I didn't hustle Walter in the other direction, he was angry enough to kill Simon with his bare hands."

Sonia stroked her chin. "If Simon stole Walter's line, maybe he pushed Walter past his breaking point."

Hope scratched the crown of her head. "Is having Simon steal his line a strong enough motive for Walter to *kill* the guy?"

I shrugged. "I dunno. In this industry, it's not uncommon for lines to be stolen by one rep from another." I raised my coffee cup to Hope. "Even though it was obvious Walter had a big burr up his butt for Simon, you're right, it's a stretch he'd *murder the guy* over a stolen line."

Sonia dipped her head. "People murder over less..."

Queenie rolled her eyes. "It doesn't matter how hot the product is, it's a helluva lot easier to replace the stolen line than risk spending the rest of your days in prison over the if-come-maybe you *might get a big order* if you got the hot line back."

Joan funneled her lips. "The twins?"

I squeaked as loud as a trapped mouse. "*Lauren and Lucinda*?"

"Yes, *Lauren and Lucinda*." Joan rolled her eyes. "Who else? The Olsen twins?"

I shook my head. "I dunno, Joan. They are two grounded, down-to-earth women."

Hope wrinkled her nose as if she had just taken a big whiff of yesterday's garbage. "Perhaps, but *Simon extorted Lucinda to put out on command* as the price tag for a pay raise she was entitled to, for crying out loud."

Joan laughed. "If Lucinda were the killer, she'd be acquitted by a jury."

Queenie pursed her lips. "Only if it were an all-female jury."

Once herself a victim of extortion that led to a wrongful murder arrest, Sonia's eyes turned as dark as the inside of a witch's cauldron. "If your back is against the wall and you have no other options, anyone is capable of murder."

Queenie tsked. "She had an option. Quit her job and work somewhere else."

I shook my head. "Besides, the killer was inside the fashion show theater. The twins were a no-show."

Joan mused, "The place was packed. Just because you didn't see them doesn't mean they weren't in the building."

Sonia asked, "Anyone else?"

I raised my index finger. "Avril Wilts. She's my number one suspect choice. She's got motive out of the wazoo. She despised Simon for trying to steal her job three times, including twice while at this market. She revealed the horrible things he pulled on her, including blackmail and extortion, and the lengths she'd go to stop him. Avril and I were walking together on the way to the trade show arena on the first day of the market when she spied Simon in her booth, talking to the owners of her company. She said, '*I worked my ass off to get where I am. If the slug is trying to take it away from me, I swear to God I'll kill him.*' The night of the fashion show, Avril was busy buttonholing Mariel, but when she saw Simon cozying up to her bosses again, she raced over to them to make sure Simon hadn't succeeded in taking her job." I steepled my fingers. "It's not a big leap for her to make good on her threat."

Sonia asked, "And the means?"

Queenie grinned. "Her remarkable purse converted into boots or stilettos. But if it was empty, the interior could hold either a weekend's wardrobe, a small swimwear presentation, or, in a pinch, a bowling ball." Queenie splayed her fingers. "The coconut was smaller than a bowling ball, so it would fit inside the purse."

Hope scratched her head. "Wasn't Mariel the one who had the Brazilian cocktail served in the coconut?"

I nodded. "You're right."

Hope asked, "So, how did Avril get it?" Hope wrinkled her nose. "Did she ask Mariel for a sip of her drink and didn't give the coconut back?"

I shook my head. "No, but Avril somehow managed to manipulate the seating arrangement so she and her bosses sat next to my mother and Mariel inside the theater. At the end of the fashion show, Mariel, Avril, her bosses, and my mother walked out of the theater together into the lobby. My mother said Mariel threw the coconut into a trash container in the lobby. Let's say that Avril watched where Mariel discarded the coconut. Maybe Avril said good night to the group and doubled back when the lobby was empty. Say she took the coconut out of the trash can and stashed it in her purse. What if Avril noticed Simon at the fashion show and followed him up to the storage room on the pretext of fetching her samples? Or they went up together, argued, and it got out of hand. Avril wasn't at all shy about expressing her anger with Mariel for not placing any Tigress Swimwear orders. If she killed Simon, Mariel was the perfect patsy to frame for the crime. In my book, Avril is the hands-down winner in the murder derby. She checks all the boxes for the big three." I held up three fingers. "Motive. Means. Opportunity."

"In theory, it's game-set-match," Queenie smirked. "Now, Miss Marple, let's see you prove it."

Before I replied with my snappy retort, my cell phone rang again.

Mo Lehrman.

Some things never change.

He was always persistent.

Once, it was exhilarating.

This time, I didn't care.

Queenie pointed to my phone. "That's the third call you didn't answer. If it's a wrong number, take the call and tell them they have the wrong number. Otherwise, they will keep calling and wasting their time and yours."

I pursed my lips. "It's someone I once considered important but isn't anymore and doesn't deserve the courtesy I'd give to a wrong number dialer."

Chapter Twenty-Three

Every booth station was occupied. Harriet and I worked together with Greg Wellford, CEO of Elvira's Beachcomber Shops from Pensacola. With a fifty-store chain spanning the Florida Panhandle from Jacksonville to Mobile, this was a key account with a big pencil that carried all our divisions. The meeting was a long one that started at noon, and Greg was in our booth until almost 3:30.

We finally got a break in the action at 3:45. Breakfast seemed like it was a week ago. I was famished. I took half of a dried-out tuna on rye, the last sandwich on the caterer's tray, a diet soda from the mini fridge, and collapsed into a chair. I gobbled the sandwich in six bites and took a big swig of soda to wash it down.

I checked the time. It was 4:00 in Miami and 1:00 in LA. Buddy was probably on his way back from lunch.

I looked over at Lauren. "When is the next appointment?"

"Half an hour."

I gave her the OK sign and picked up my cell phone. There were twelve messages from Mo. I deleted them all and dialed Buddy's cell phone number. One ring. Two rings. Three rings. Four rings. Voicemail. Insecurity squeezed my heart. Was Buddy avoiding me like I was avoiding Mo? Nah. It was a punishment meted out by a guilty conscience for a night of lust. What was the chance of *that* happening again? Elephants would sooner fly.

I waited for his greeting to end and made what I hoped was a cheery message. "Hi, Sweetheart. It's me. I'm between appointments and hoped we could chat for a few minutes. I'm sorry I missed you. I hope that you're having a good day. I'll try to call again later."

Just as I cooed, "Miss you, baby. Can't wait to see you..." Mo Lehrman stormed into the booth.

From the daggers of anger shooting from his eyes, the detective must have caught the last part of my message. Good. Stick the knife in a little deeper, Schlivnik. I bit back the evil laugh on the tip of my tongue.

I flattened my voice to a disinterested monotone. "Good afternoon, Detective Lehrman. Are you here on official police business?"

Mo looked at me oddly. "What are you talking about?"

He shook his head the same way Siggie does if he doesn't understand something. "Why didn't you return any of my calls?"

I said, "This isn't the time or place to discuss it. If you're not here on official police business, I'm expecting a customer momentarily, and you'll have to excuse me."

He crossed his arms akimbo over his chest and huffed, "I'm not leaving without an answer."

Too many tongues already wagged over the soap opera my love life had suddenly become. I'd be damned if I'd give them an encore performance.

"Fine. But we are not doing this in the booth." I grabbed him by the shirt sleeve and pulled him through the booth door. I turned to face Queenie. "Cover for me. I'll be back as soon as I take care of this. Call the cops if I'm not back in an hour..." I glanced at Mo and giggled, "Oops, never mind."

The convention center was far from a convenient place for a private conversation. The booths and restrooms were out, and so was the lobby. The loading dock? Nah. Too hot. Too noisy. Too crowded. A conference room would have been perfect...if I had a key. That late, the food court was probably the least crowded place in the building.

Surprisingly, a handful of food vendors were still open. Customers were scattered throughout the circular venue, but there were several vacant sections. We sat across from each other at a Formica-topped table for two in uncomfortable plastic chairs.

Mo tipped his hand as though drinking from a cup. "How about a coffee or a soda?"

I shook my head. "We won't be here that long."

He made a sour face. "Okay, then let's get to it. Why didn't you return any of my calls?"

I shrugged. "I had nothing to say to you."

His jaw dropped. "You purposely ignored *twelve* phone calls, and *that's* your reason? Give me something more. If you're angry with me, tell me what I did so I can fix it."

I shook my head. "It can't be fixed."

"Anything can be fixed."

I put my hand over my heart. "Not a broken heart."

His mouth gaped open. "I *broke your heart*? How? When did I have the time to break it? I left you in the morning, and we both went to our jobs. We were only apart for a few hours..."

A glimmer of recognition shone in his eyes.

He folded his arms across his chest. "So, let me get this straight. You're angry with me *for doing my job*?"

Your crackerjack reasoning skills are amazing, Detective.

"You played me for a fool. You betrayed me."

"How?"

"The night before, you had already decided to arrest Mariel, but you didn't say anything."

He held out his hands. "For what it's worth, I didn't have sufficient evidence to make the arrest that night. I only interviewed the three witnesses after I left you in the morning. But even if I had decided to arrest her the night before, I couldn't have said anything."

"I'm no stranger. You could have said something."

"You're right, you're not a stranger. But you are a *witness* with both a personal and professional relationship with the suspect. So, discussing any part of an ongoing investigation with a witness in the same case would cost me my badge, especially if the witness inadvertently or purposely gave the suspect a heads up."

My back stiffened. "I would *never* do that. But the worst thing was that you questioned my mother's honesty and integrity. You took the word of *three strangers* who had a reason to lie over my mother's. I can't get past that. I'm sorry."

His eyes widened. "You eavesdropped on my interrogation?"

I smirked. "Is eavesdropping a crime? Am I under arrest?" I held out my hands. "Are you going to cuff me like you did Mariel Levine?" My zingers dripped sarcasm. "If I ask nicely, can you arrange for Mariel and me to have adjoining cells so we can chat?"

"Don't make light of a situation as serious as an arrest. Depriving anyone of their freedom is something every policeman does with a heavy heart."

I rolled my eyes. "Bullpucky. You weren't exactly broken up as the uniform slapped the handcuffs on Mariel." I stood up. "Okay, I answered your question. I've got nothing more to say to you except goodbye."

I stood and walked away. He ran after me. "Are you crazy? *Goodbye*? The other night was a new beginning for us, not the end."

"The other night was nothing more than lust, not love. It was a mistake. It meant nothing. And it won't happen again."

I moved. He countered. I changed directions. So did he.

I sighed. "Get out of my way, Mo."

He shook his head and stood his ground.

I pushed his chest, but I might as well have tried moving a mountain. I raised my voice, and it echoed loudly around the nearly-empty venue. "*I said, get out of my way*!"

Walter Seiden appeared out of thin air and wedged his body between Mo and me. "Holly, is this clown bothering you?"

Mo flipped out his badge and shoved it under Walter's nose. "This is a private conversation. Mind your own business and move along."

Walter stood his ground. "Only if the lady says so."

I glared at Mo. "Detective Lehrman was just leaving, *right*?"

Mo held his hands up and gritted his teeth. "For now, yes. But this conversation isn't over. I won't let us...We can't...end everything this way."

My eyes filled watching him stalk out of the food court. Was he out of my life? That's what I said I wanted. But is it? What have I done?

Chapter Twenty-Four

If the two gloating apparitions had shown up, that would have just put the cherry on the sundae. I was relieved they didn't. But Marie LaValle was too determined a woman to give up without a fight. It begged the question, what was she up to?

Walter touched my arm, and I jumped. "You okay?"

I shrugged.

He pulled out a chair. "Take a seat. I'll get us a couple of coffees. A few sips of some strong java and you'll snap right back."

If only it were that simple.

I mouthed a thank you and sat down.

Walter returned a few minutes later and pushed a cup of steaming hot coffee in front of me. He dropped a handful of packaged powdered cream and sugar between us. He smiled self-consciously. "I forgot to ask how you take your coffee."

I smiled. "*No problema, señor*. I drink it black."

Walter gave me an odd look. "You speak Spanish?"

I nodded. "Since over half of my employees are Spanish speakers, speaking Spanish is essential."

He pursed his lips. "I don't interact with any non-English speakers."

I pointed to a group of Spanish-speaking loading dock workers on break, seated two tables away from us.

"There are almost two million Spanish speakers who live in the Miami-Dade area alone. It is impossible to avoid interaction with someone who speaks Spanish."

He shrugged.

Walter dipped his head to the exit. "He's the detective on the Posnick case, right? A different policeman interviewed me, but I recognized Lehrman's name as the detective in charge of the investigation on the paperwork I was given to sign."

I nodded. "Yes, he is."

Walter said, "Not to be nosy, but you and the cop are...together?"

"We were a long time ago. We hadn't seen one another until recently. Why do you ask?"

Walter blushed as red as a tomato and found something fascinating about his shoelaces. "My wife was diagnosed with cervical cancer. She died two years ago."

I squeezed his hand. "I'm so sorry for your loss."

His eyes filled. "By the time the cancer was discovered, it was too late. She fought like hell, but she suffered. She died a horrible death, so her passing was a blessing. The first few months, I barely functioned." He twisted the gold wedding band on his ring finger. "Life without her was unimaginable. I prayed for my death, but God paid no attention. The only thing keeping me going was that she wanted me to go on. She made me promise not to live the rest of my life alone." He stuttered like a shy teenager trying to ask a girl to the prom. "I-It's probably s-silly, b-but I-I...m-maybe you'd go out to d-dinner with me."

"My evenings are all taken with entertaining customers, but I'll see if I can move some things around." I squeezed his hand to soften the blow. "But Walter, *only as friends*. A long-distance relationship is not in the cards. It's the primary reason things didn't work out with Mo Lehrman. So, if two friends breaking bread together works for you, okay. If not, I understand, but I'll pass."

He nodded.

"The word around the trade show is that you and your business partner discovered Posnick's body." Walter shuddered. "How utterly awful."

"We did, and it was gruesome. This wasn't a murder. It was an act of rage." I shuddered. "Whoever killed him hated Simon with a capital H."

Walter looked at me oddly. "Why do you say *whoever killed him*? Your friend, the detective, arrested Mariel Levine for the crime."

I nodded. "True. But she's not the one whodunit."

Walter scrunched up his nose. "If the police arrested her, they must have the evidence. If *they*'re convinced it was Mariel, why do *you* question it? Mariel is a nice person, but sometimes if they are pushed too far, even good people are capable of doing terrible things."

I smiled as the voice of LAPD Homicide Detective A.J. Yakamura repeated Walter's words inside my head. "A friend in LA once said the same thing. Nonetheless, my gut says Mariel isn't the killer."

Walter said, "Well, in this country, you're innocent until proven guilty. So, I guess a jury will decide one way or another."

"If it gets that far. There is no shortage of potential suspects. Let's face it, Simon Posnick was not a popular guy. A lot of people, *including you*, Walter, shed no tears when Simon bought the farm."

Walter pursed his lips. "I had my issues with the guy. No question about it. But the cops are convinced Mariel's issue was much bigger than mine or anyone else's."

I shrugged. "Time will tell."

We finished our coffee and started back to our booths.

Walter glanced at his watch. "It's almost closing time. Do you need a ride to your hotel? I'm happy to help. It's too hot and humid outside to stand in the queue waiting for a cab."

I shook my head. "Thanks for the offer. My group and I are staying at the Caribe Royal. It's only two blocks from the convention center, so we hoof it."

Walter said, "The place is supposed to be magnificent. My cousin and his wife stayed at the hotel when it reopened. They loved the Art

Deco lobby, but went over the moon with the rooftop garden. Have you been up there?"

I shook my head. "No, but you're the second person to rave about it, so I will check it out before we leave town. The hotel also has a private beach near the boardwalk. I am an early bird and a walker. Since the hotel is on Collins Avenue, I take turns between the beach and the street for my morning constitutionals."

As we turned the corner to the booths, we stopped before Walter's. He craned his neck to see if Avril was in her booth. Walter sighed with relief. "Thank God Avril isn't around. Since the murder, she's been behaving even weirder."

The woman growls like a tiger. How much weirder could she possibly get?

"What's she doing?"

"You know how much she complained about Mariel?"

She never missed an opportunity.

I nodded.

"Well, since the murder, now all she does is sing Mariel's praises. What do you make of it?"

"Avril had her issues with Simon. If Mariel did it, Avril is celebrating that Mariel beat her to the punch."

Or, Avril Wilts punched Simon's ticket and framed Mariel Levine for the deed, and she is celebrating her getting away with murder.

I thanked Walter for the coffee and for coming to my rescue, and we parted company.

I wasn't ready to face the Yentas and their barrage of well-meaning questions of concern. I texted Queenie that I was done for the day. I went back to the hotel and indulged myself with a pity party. A bubble bath and room service were the guests of honor.

Chapter Twenty-Five

The bubble bath and a split of Chardonnay to wash down my lobster quesadilla eased the sting of my confrontation with Mo, but a combination of confusion and heartache kept me up most of the night, tossing and turning.

At six o'clock, I threw in the towel and pulled on a tank top and shorts, and stepped into my sneakers. I took a pre-dawn walk on hot and humid Collins Avenue. I strolled to the end of the Lincoln Road pedestrian mall and back to sweat the cobwebs out and clear my head from yesterday's humdinger set of events. I got back to my room an hour later and didn't want to be alone with my angst. But it was too early to see if the Yentas were up for a cuppa and conversation.

The only person on the planet I could call at four o'clock in the morning without waking up out of a dead sleep is my favorite medical examiner and BFF, Dr. Sophie Cutler.

For a medical doctor, she never followed the advice she gave everyone else. Her eating habits are atrocious. Pizza, hamburgers, and rich, gooey desserts are the staples of her diet. Cottage cheese is a curse word in her vocabulary. And the explanation she gives for her ticker miraculously still pumping? She runs five miles daily before the crack of dawn as penance for her dietary sins.

I brewed a strong cuppa in the mini coffee maker in the hotel room. I gulped two restorative slugs and hit speed dial number two for Snip.

She answered on the first ring. "Good morning. This is Los Angeles County Assistant Medical Examiner Dr. Sophie Cutler. You stab 'em, and we slab 'em."

I laughed. "How did you ever survive before Caller ID?"

"It was a challenge. So, Madame Triple M, the word is you weren't in Miami seventy-two hours before someone in the swimwear industry got whacked. I bet it's a new record for your corpse-catching."

I huffed. "It's clear why a couple of wise guys like you and Jazzy were kindred spirits."

"I resemble that remark."

"If the scalpel fits..."

Snip laughed. "So, you called because you missed my rapier wit, or is something on your mind?"

"Both."

"Okay. How can I help you?"

"The homicide detective arrested the wrong suspect..."

Snip snickered. "*Of course he did.* And naturally, *you've identified the actual killer*."

"Sarcasm is so unbecoming for a woman of your stature... Putting your tacky comment aside, I don't have the proof yet, but I've got an idea who the killer is."

"Since I have no jurisdiction, other than offering an opinion on your theory, there's nothing else I can do for you this time."

"Ah, but you are wrong, Dr. Death."

"How much am I going to hate this request?"

"Compared to some of the ones I've made in the past, this one is a no-brainer. All I want you to do is to call Jazzy on my behalf and convince her to work with me the way you do."

She clucked her tongue. "Here's a novel idea. Try going directly to the source and sharing your thoughts with the detective instead?"

"Not a possibility."

"Do I want to know why?"

"Not on your life."

Recognizing that the chance of my not hounding her until either she capitulated or died of old age was zero, Snip accepted the inevitability of her defeat and sighed. "O-kay. I'll make the call. Do. Not. Make. Me. Regret. This. Do you hear me?"

"Yes, ma'am. Loud and clear. Thanks, Snip. I owe you one."

"No, you owe me hundreds, scratch that...you owe me thousands."

"Fine. Put it on my tab."

"Holly, don't do anything stupid. Stupid is the way you get dead. Try not to become one of Jazzy's patients. It's a pain in the tush to break in a new BFF. I'll ring her now before she gets too busy...or before I come to my senses."

"Funny. Like a toe tag."

Snip laughed. "Quit while you're ahead."

She didn't have to say it twice.

I made a squeaky kissy noise and hung up before she changed her mind.

I took a coolish shower and changed clothes, and was as ready as I'd ever be to face the Yentas.

I sat across from Joan and sipped my coffee. She stared me down over her eyeglasses. "Are you out on bail?"

I rolled my eyes. "The last time I checked, not returning a phone call wasn't a crime."

"So, you managed to talk your way out of the hot bowl of a mess with Detective Lehrman?"

I squirmed in my seat. "It depends upon your perspective."

"Meaning?"

"Meaning, if a budding romance was the desired outcome, then not so much. If extrication from said romance was the goal, then yes is the correct answer."

Hope's jaw dropped. "*You dumped him?*"

I winced. "Dump is such an ugly word. Let's say going forward, our relationship will be strictly professional."

Sonia asked, "Your choice, not his?"

I nodded.

Queenie gave me the once-over. "So, why do you look like you just lost your soulmate?"

Because maybe I did...

I couldn't look her in the eye. "The lobster quesadilla argued with the Chardonnay, and I was up most of last night."

Joan funneled her lips. "Bullpucky. It sounds a lot more like a case of seller's remorse than indigestion, if you ask me."

I checked the time. Eight thirty on the nose. I finished my coffee and stood. "If the skewering session is complete, shall we head to the convention center so that customers who pay for the privilege of eviscerating me can finish the job?"

Chapter Twenty-Six

I speed walked ahead of the Yentas. Queenie caught up to me as I crossed Collins Avenue. She hooked her arm into the crook of my elbow. "It might not sound like it, but the girls and I are concerned about you."

I smiled. "I know. As Nana always said, 'This too shall pass...'"

"Is that what you want?"

I shrugged. "I thought I did. Now? I dunno. I guess I'll play it out and see how things go."

"Part of the concern was you were gone for *such a long time...*"

"I ought to be flattered. He wouldn't let me go...literally."

"How do you mean, literally? He wasn't accepting the breakup, or he physically wouldn't let you go?"

"Both."

She gave me the big eyes. "*He prevented you from leaving*?"

I nodded. "Yeah, and you'll never in a million years guess which knight in shining armor came to my rescue."

Queenie shrugged. "No clue."

"Walter Seiden."

That tidbit stopped the Queenster in her tracks. "*Shut up*!"

I held up my right hand. "If I'm lyin', I'm dyin'. He appeared out of thin air and got between Mo and me. He asked if, and I quote, *Is this clown bothering you, Holly*?"

Queenie burst out laughing. "And how quickly did the dynamic detective pull out his gun?"

I grinned. "No gun, but he whipped his badge out faster than you could say you're under arrest. He told Walter we were having a private conversation and to move along."

"So, Walter retreated?"

I shook my head. "Nope. He held his ground and said he'd only back off if the lady wanted him to. I lasered Mo with my death ray stare and said *Detective Lehrman was leaving*. Mo reluctantly left...but not before promising the conversation wasn't over."

"So, once Mo was gone, why didn't you come back to the booth?"

"I guess I looked a little shaky, and Walter insisted I join him for coffee. Since Walter is on our suspect list, I figured it was an opportunity to kill two birds with one stone, so I agreed."

"Did you get anything of value out of the conversation?"

I twisted my wrist back and forth. "No smoking gun. He readily admitted his issues with Simon but was quick to say the police said Mariel's were bigger than anyone else's, including his. I said Mariel wasn't the killer, and he gave me the canned response of *If it's good enough for the cops, why isn't it good enough for me?*"

"So, it sounds as if you got a cup of coffee and little else out of the conversation."

"No. As it turned out, I got a lot. We got to his booth, and he craned his neck to see if Avril Wilts was in hers. She wasn't, and Walter was relieved."

"What's his beef with Avril?"

"Their booths are next to one another's, and she constantly complained about Mariel."

"Walter had better get in the boat and row. Did he say anything else?"

I nodded. "Yeah. Since Simon's murder, Avril is now singing Mariel's praises for killing him."

Queenie narrowed her eyes. "What do you make of that?"

"Walter asked the same question. Either she is grateful Mariel beat her to it. Or if I'm right, and Avril is the killer, it's a celebration that her framing of Mariel was successful."

We entered the convention center entrance, and I said, "Go on down to the booth. I'm going to pay a visit to Avril and confront her about her lies."

Queenie warned me with a wag of her index finger. "Be careful the way you couch your questions. If she's the killer, she'll do anything to keep Mariel as the suspect. Including killing you to shut you up. Don't do anything stupid. Remember..."

I waved her off. "Yeah, yeah. Stupid is the way I get myself killed." I held out my hands. "No more girls' nights out for you and Snip together. You're beginning to quote one another's lines."

Queenie gave me the middle finger salute, and we went our separate ways. Five minutes later, I arrived at Avril's booth. She wasn't there, but a buxom blonde wearing a string bikini, leaving little to the imagination, stood posing in the center of the booth.

I stuck my head in. "Excuse me, is Avril around?"

The blonde shook her head. "Sorry, she's not."

"Will she be back soon?"

She shrugged. "No idea. She drove the Larsens to the airport. If the traffic on the 836 isn't jammed, I imagine she'll be back in an hour." She walked up to the front of the booth and read my name on the plastic vendor ID attached to a lanyard hanging around my neck. "I'll tell her you stopped by, Holly."

The element of surprise and catching Avril off guard was critical. "Nah." I waved her off. "I'll be in and out today. I'll pop over later. Thanks anyway."

She shrugged, and I moved on to Walter's booth. Remarkably, I struck out again. His model said he took a legal pad and pen and had been gone for half an hour.

I approached our booth and glanced across the aisle to Simon's. Walter Seiden was in the booth with Lucinda. She was holding up samples, and he was taking notes as if going over the line. Huh?

I stuck my head inside Simon's booth. "Walter, are you lost?" I pointed to the end of the aisle. "You're two aisles down from us, remember?"

Walter flashed a hundred-thousand-watt grin. "Nope. I'm not lost. I got the line back and am going over the styles with Lucinda."

Walter certainly wasted no time. Simon's body was barely cold.

Luce looked up and waved hello, and I did a double-take. The ugly black and purple shiner was now a smudged pale-yellow shadow. The outline of the large hand imprinted on her cheek was gone, and her lower lip was no longer swollen. The cuts, bruises, and scratches on her lower arms were barely visible.

"You cleaned up nicely, girl!"

Luce patted her cheeks. "The Frankenstein look wasn't too attractive. Antibiotics, antiseptic cream, and a bucketful of industrial-strength make-up concealers work miracles." She stretched her arm to reach a sample and winced. "I'm still not ready to run a marathon, but at least all my parts are moving the way they're supposed to."

"Any updates from the police?"

Luce's eyes clouded over. "Nothing. The detective gave me little hope the bastard would ever be caught."

"You scratched the guy's arm and the side of his face, right?"

She nodded.

"How about his DNA under your fingernails?"

Luce shrugged. "I asked. The detective said the lab ran it through their statewide system, but there wasn't a match. He said if the attacker had no police record, nothing would be in the system to match the skin under my nails." Her voice caught. "The bastard's going to get away Scot free."

I bit my lower lip. "Maybe not."

Her voice rose to a squeak. "How can you say that?"

"Simon Posnick's arm and side of his face had big scratches on them the night of the fashion show."

She shook her head. "It wasn't Simon."

"Tell the detective anyway. You can't be so sure. You were upset, and understandably so. If you were thinking more clearly, you'd recognize something to identify him. The police lab will get Simon's DNA from the coroner and compare it to the skin under your fingernails."

Luce tsked, "Even if they match and it turns out to be Simon, so what? He's dead and will never pay for what he did."

"If Simon was the attacker, at least you won't be looking over your shoulder for the rest of your life, always worrying that the attacker could come back and finish what he started. Tell the detective. Let him and the lab decide whether or not it's too late to ID the perp."

She nodded. "Okay, Hol. I will."

I turned to Walter. "Is Luce working the rest of the market for you with this line in Simon's booth, or are you moving the samples to yours?"

He shook his head. "No. For continuity and convenience, I'm leaving the line in this booth, and Lucinda will work all the appointments Simon scheduled. The company sent out a letter to all of Simon's accounts announcing the change in salesmen. Lucinda messaged all the retailers with appointments during the time the booth was dark and is rescheduling as many as possible for the rest of the market."

I turned to Lucinda. "Luce, before you leave for the day, stop by our booth so you, Harriet, Lauren, and I can brainstorm about your next gig."

Lucinda lightly cuffed Walter's chin. "Walter offered me the job of his showroom manager at the Miami Merchandise Mart, and I accepted."

I clapped. “Fantastic news. Congratulations.”

Walter said, “Since being in the mart and on the road at the same time is impossible, Lucinda will run the showroom.”

I nodded. “A win-win.”

I waved goodbye and crossed the aisle to our booth.

Chapter Twenty-Seven

I bit my tongue not to laugh as Jazzy polished off the last slice of The Kitchen Sink, the house special of Mastriano's Little Pizza Heaven at the tip of Sunny Isles Beach. The server refilled our wine glasses and asked if we cared for dessert. I was stuffed and declined, but Jazzy insisted we share a piece of Torta di Ricotta e Mascarpone cheesecake and a short order of espresso coffee.

I drained my Chianti and grinned. "Eating dinner with you is the same as eating with Snip. No wonder you two were like peas in a pod at medical school." I clucked my tongue. "Since you share the same atrocious eating habits, do you run five miles a day before dawn to atone for your food sins the way she does?"

Jazzy put her hand over her heart and grimaced. "Heck no. I'd never do anything so boring."

"I agree. But, your metabolism must be super to eat the same way as Snip and not look like the broad side of a barn."

Jazzy held her hands up and made two fists. "Nope. My metabolism is normal. I'm a devoted kickboxer. I work my daily routine from six to seven at a woman's kickboxing gym around the corner from the morgue. It's great aerobic exercise and a fantastic stress buster." She asked, "Since you're in the bikini biz, are you a swimmer?"

I held my hands out. "To tell you the truth, I'm around swimsuits twenty-four-seven, so the *last thing* I want to do is wear one. The closest I get to swimming is living at the beach on a houseboat. My standard poodle and I walk a daily three-mile round-trip from our marina to the Washington Street pier before dawn."

Jazzy's eyes lit. "Living on a houseboat sounds wonderful. I'm a water woman too. I live in a bungalow at Surfside across the bay from Bal Harbor."

I said, "I hope it was okay asking Snip to intercede on my behalf. Cutting to the chase, in my opinion, Mo arrested the wrong suspect. I have an idea who the killer is, but I need help proving it. Snip and I have worked on a few cases and had good results. Since you don't know me from a hole in the wall, I figured a recommendation from her gave me credibility."

Jazzy grinned. "Sophie spoke quite highly of you and your...how did she put it...oh yeah...your *tenacity*."

"So, lemme translate. You might as well agree to work with me because otherwise, I will annoy you to death."

Jazzy laughed. "Yeah. That pretty much summed it up in a nutshell."

"Have you completed the autopsy on Simon Posnick yet?"

"Yep. Two hours ago."

"Does Mo have the report yet?"

"Yes. I faxed it to him before leaving for the day."

"And did you also fax a copy to Mariel Levine's attorney?"

"Absolutely."

I turned my head sideways and touched the back of my head at the spot where my skull met the upper base of my neck. "My fingers are at the place where the jagged edge of the coconut shell was jammed into Simon's head. Did the coconut kill him, or was his death caused by something else?"

Jazzy reminded me of Snip as she donned her professor's cap. "The brainstem is made up of the midbrain, pons, and medulla. It is located between the diencephalon, which is the thalamus and hypothalamus region, and the spinal cord."

"Sorry, I missed that lecture in med school."

She grinned and pointed to my finger at the back of my head. "The spinal cord begins at the base of the brainstem. All connections between the brain and the body must travel through the brainstem. The brainstem plays a vital role in regulating consciousness and in the critical functions of heart rate and breathing. The tip of the jagged edge of the coconut was sharp. A strong downward motion thrust the tip of the coconut into the intersection of the brainstem and the spinal cord and severed them."

I said, "We found Simon's corpse prone, lying on its stomach. Which position was he in when the blow was struck?"

"He was standing."

"So, if it was a downward thrust, the killer is tall, right?"

Jazzy nodded.

I hovered my hand over my head. "How tall?"

"The estimated range is from five feet ten inches to six feet three inches."

I flexed my muscles. "The killer was fit."

Jazzy nodded. "Yes. Since Mr. Posnick was a tall, physically fit, healthy man, the killer required upper body strength, strong arms, and powerful legs to overpower him."

"So the killer probably worked out?"

"I'd say so."

"How far in did the coconut tip penetrate?"

"The tip was thrust completely into the point of entry."

"How far in is that?"

"Approximately one point five nine millimeters."

"In inches?"

"A sixteenth of an inch."

I pinched my lips. "Did Simon suffer?"

Jazzy shook her head. "Death was virtually instantaneous. It was as if a lit lamp was plugged into an electric socket, and suddenly the power cord was severed."

Jazzy quirked a lopsided grin. "One interesting but not necessarily important tidbit is that the victim had sex the day of his demise."

I laughed. "So, he went out with a bang." I bit my lip. "As amusing as the information is, it might be the key to identifying the killer."

"How?"

"Two women despised him. One, he worked for a while back and had an affair with her that didn't end well when he tried to steal her job. The other one currently worked for him. She recently asked for a well-deserved, overdue raise. Simon extorted her to have sex with him in exchange for the salary increase. She and her twin sister, who is our showroom manager, were MIA for a pre-fashion show dinner I invited them to attend. And the twins weren't seen at the fashion show. If I give you their names, will you check to see if either of the women he was involved with went to the hospital or called the police to report a rape?"

Jazzy pulled a cell phone out of her purse and gave me an expectant look. "All I need is a name and the date."

"Lucinda Burke—with an e at the end of Burke—and Avril Wilts. Check this past Saturday or Sunday."

She tapped a few keys. "I'm in the state database. There's nothing on Lucinda Burke or Avril Wilts. I've widened the search date to today, but nothing on either name appeared from Saturday through today. I'm sorry."

I smacked a fist into the palm of my hand. "Dammit. I was so sure one of them was Simon's willing or unwilling sex partner that night."

Jazzy funneled her lips. "Just because it wasn't reported doesn't mean it didn't happen. The stigma still exists for rape that somehow it's the victim's fault, so the rate of cases never reported is suspected to be high. And if one were willing, there would be nothing to report."

"Maybe Avril, the one he worked for years ago, lured Simon into the storage room with the promise of renewing their sexual relationship, or said she was going to the storage room to retrieve her samples, and invited him to accompany her. The day after the fashion show, Lucinda came to work bruised and battered from an attack behind the convention center. She said she was unable to identify her attacker. She said it wasn't Simon and that she wasn't raped. But maybe she lied. I'm leaning in that direction. The only way to determine if either of them was Simon's sex partner is to confront them." I twisted my lips into a wry smile. "The only woman *not* Simon's possible sex partner is Mariel Levine."

The waiter chose that moment to serve the cheesecake and coffee. My stomach roiled at the description of Simon's death, and the pizza meal threatened an encore appearance. Dessert and coffee were fated for a doggie bag and a takeaway cup.

Jazzy, on the other hand, dove into her cheesecake with the gusto of a true dessert connoisseur. Oblivious to my discomfort, Jazzy smacked her lips and made short work of her cheesecake and washed it down with two big sips of coffee. She eyed my uneaten portion and made a guiltless offer. "If you're still too full, I'll split it with you."

I pushed the plate across the table. "Be my guest."

Jazzy hacked off half and scooted it onto her plate, and pushed the rest back to me.

I asked, "Was the killer right or left-handed?"

Jazzy picked up a knife with her left hand and held it over her head. She arced downward and jabbed the tip into the piece of cheesecake. "From the angle of the entry wound, the killer was left-handed."

"Have you determined the sex of the killer?"

"Not yet." Jazzy held a hand above her head. "The killer could be either a tall woman or an average-height to a tall man."

I held out a ta-da with my hands. "Based on your findings, it's impossible for Mariel Levine to be the killer. Mariel is a middle-aged woman, no more than five feet four, and she is right-handed. Avril Wilts is young, tall, fit, works out, and is left-handed. And she had big issues with both Simon and Mariel. She made the issues public, and as often as possible. Two others fit the height range. They also had beefs with Simon, but none with Mariel. Avril Wilts checks all the boxes. If I were a betting woman, Avril is the one I'd put money on."

Jazzy typed several notes into her smartphone. "Detective Lehrman and Ms. Levine's counsel will be informed of the height and hand attributes of the killer based on the physical details of the entry wound with an addendum to the autopsy." Jazzy ran her fingers through her hair. "I'm only the corpse cutter, not a cop. I*nterpreting the information to determine any suspect's guilt or innocence* is not in my purview. Discuss the issue of guilt or innocence with the detective."

I pursed my lips. "Not a possibility."

"Why not?"

"I'm not speaking to him at the moment."

Chapter Twenty-Eight

Jazzy dropped me off at the hotel around nine. I left a message with Lo-Lo's answering service. Twenty minutes later, I sat across from her in the hotel lobby bar, sharing a bottle of Merlot and the Assistant Coroner's information.

I finished giving the recap of my conversation with Jazzy and asked, "Is it enough to get the charges against Mariel dropped?"

Lo-Lo bit her lower lip. "Probably, but I'll need the written addendum to present to the court, along with the original autopsy report itself."

"Is the fact that Simon had sex the day of his murder a help or a harm for Mariel?"

"A help. Ms. Levine wouldn't be a willing partner. She exhibited no signs of having been raped. If she were raped, she would have claimed it as her alibi if she indeed had killed Mr. Posnick. My argument will be that, based on Dr. Jones' analysis of how the murder weapon was inserted into the victim's brainstem with a downward arc, unless she stood on stilts, it is *physically impossible* for Mariel Levine to have committed the crime. Ms. Levine was arraigned, which means the charges against her were read in court, and she entered a plea of not guilty. But she has not been indicted, and based on the addendum, she probably won't be. Detective Lehrman may contest my filing. If he does, it might delay things as the judge will give him time to make his case. But since he'll receive the same information from the ME as I will, Detective Lehrman will be hard-pressed to convince the court not to grant my request."

She smiled. "Auntie Ro said you were a pistol." Lo-Lo raised her glass in a toast. "I disagree. You're a freakin' machine gun. You ought to consider saying bye-bye to the bikini biz and becoming a private investigator."

I burst out laughing. "The concept alone would result in mass resignations at several LAPD precincts."

"Well, if you ever decide to change careers and move back to Miami, I'd hire you as my investigator in a minute."

I held out my hands. "I appreciate the offer, but I love my life in LA as it is now."

We polished off the Merlot with a toast to the charges against Mariel being dropped. Lo-Lo held her wineglass high. "Thanks to you, this may be the fastest I've ever gotten a client off."

I bowed from the waist. "I live to serve."

I pointed to Heaven. "As my Nana always said, from your lips to God's ears."

I waited with her until the parking valet brought her car to the front of the hotel. Lo-Lo slid into the driver's seat, rolled the window down, and called out, "I'll call you from court."

It was well past the time to call and not scare the panties off my mother, but I called her anyway. She could use some good news. She surprised me by answering on the first ring.

"Mom?"

"You were expecting somebody else?"

"No, it's late, and I'm surprised you're still up."

"If you thought I was asleep, why did you call? Are you disappointed you didn't wake me?"

I laughed. "No. I'm glad you're up. I could have waited until the morning, but I figured it's never too late to share good news."

She sighed. "You're not kidding. Mariel had better get released soon. There aren't enough hours in the day for me to do her job and mine. I brought work home *again*. That's the reason I'm still up. So, let's hear the good news."

"I ate dinner tonight with Jazzy Jones, the assistant Miami-Dade medical examiner, who, by the way, is a medical school colleague of Sophie's. Dr. Jones performed Simon Posnick's autopsy and shared some of the details, and surprise, surprise: Based on the height and dominant hand of the killer, Mariel is physically incapable of killing Simon."

Mom yelped, "Hallelujah! How fast will she be out of jail?"

"I dunno. I met with Ms. Lowenstein about an hour ago and gave her all the details. Ms. Lowenstein thinks it's enough to get the charges dropped. Once she receives the addendum autopsy documents, she will file them with the court and request that the charges be dropped. If she has all the documentation, gets to see the judge, and the judge agrees, Mariel could be released in the next few days. Ms. Lowenstein expected Mo to fight it, which might delay Mariel's release."

Mom groaned. "Crap! Are the chances high that he'll prevail?"

"According to Ms. Lowenstein, slimsky to nonesky."

"Okay. Let's hope she's right. Thanks for the good news. I might get a few winks of sleep tonight."

"Good. Love ya, Mom."

"Love ya more, kiddo."

Chapter Twenty-Nine

I finished my recap of the festivities of the night before, and Joan telegraphed the insidious smirk of hers that she flashes whenever a snarky comment is on the tip of her tongue. Sure enough, she wound up and zinged me with one of her best. "Congratulations, Madame Triple M. This is a first. You cleared the wrongly accused in record-breaking time, *and no one else bought the farm.*"

"No one else croaked *yet.*" Queenie held up her watch. "But the day is young. Give her time."

I took the mature approach and stuck my tongue out at Queenie. She, of course, responded with a middle finger salute. Touche.

Hope said, "So, you can hang up your sleuthing hat, Ms. Marple." She raised her coffee cup in a toast. "Good job."

Sonia rubbed her chin. "Technically, she got no one off the hook *yet*. She only set the action in motion. Until Mariel's attorney gets the judge to issue the ruling ordering the charges against her client to be dropped, nothing has changed."

I nodded. "Sonia's right. We're in a holding pattern and have no cause to celebrate yet."

I turned to Hope. "But, even if the charges are dropped, and Mariel is released, my sleuthing hat will stay on my head because..."

A chorus of synchronized groans interrupted the rest of my sentence.

Queenie rolled her eyes. "Because you have a death wish and can't mind your own beeswax to save your life."

I tsked. "No, Miss Smarty Pants, I don't have a death wish. But if it happened to Simon Posnick, it could happen to any of us. So, as long as the real killer is at large, no one is safe."

Joan sucked in her cheeks. "How about taking a new approach, Miss Marple, and let the detective do his job and *detect*?"

I clucked my tongue. "Yeah, look how great *his approach* worked out the first time...not. The *detective* had a burr up his butt to close the case quickly. He *didn't detect* too much before he arrested Mariel on, at best, shaky circumstantial evidence. So, how do I trust him not to do an encore?"

Queenie sighed. "So, since you're determined to stick your nose in every place it doesn't belong, let's hear your game plan."

"I'm going to confront Avril Wilts about her and her bosses lying to Mo. She's done a dandy job of avoiding me since Mariel was arrested, and it begs the question why."

Hope asked, "If the charges are dropped and Mariel is released, does it still matter?"

I nodded. "Yes, by lying, Avril destroyed Mariel's alibi and framed her for the murder. And there is only one reason for her to lie that makes any sense..."

Sonia tapped a teaspoon rat-a-tat-tat on the edge of the table. "If you're right, Avril is the killer."

Bingo. Bongo. Jackpot. We have a winner, ladies and gentlemen. Give the girl a cigar.

Queenie waved her index finger in my face. "Try not to be the next one to buy the farm."

Joan wrinkled her nose. "So, Avril is your *only suspect*?"

"I'd bet my boat that she did it. She checks off every box. But at this point, without a smoking gun, no suspect can be eliminated. Even ones I'd be heartbroken if it proved to be them."

The Yentas chorused, "Who?"

"Lauren and Lucinda."

Queenie gasped. "*The twins*? Come on, Hol. Seriously?"

I sighed. "It pains me to say it, but I am as serious as a heart attack."

Sonia slapped her cheeks. "Now *that one* sure came out of nowhere."

Hope scratched her head. "I wasn't expecting it either."

Joan narrowed her eyes. "Why the change of heart *now*? When I brought them up, you blew me off."

I steepled my fingers. "Dr. Jones revealed that Simon had sex the night of his death. I brought up Avril's and Lucinda's names as two of his willing or unwilling partners. Jazzy went into the state system to see if either of them were listed as being admitted to a hospital for either assault or rape on Sunday night. She ran the search. Neither name appeared in a statewide search from Saturday to last night.

"The twins lied about a police report and Luce being examined at the hospital. Maybe *she was raped, and Simon was the rapist.* And instead of going to the police, they decided to kill Simon instead. They sneaked into the theater, watched Mariel toss the coconut into the trash, and after the crowd dispersed, they took it. They followed Simon up to the storage room. They surprise him while he's looking for his samples. He puts up a ferocious fight, and the samples are strewn all over the room, but the girls overpower him. They pin him against the wall, and one of them impales him with the tip of the coconut shell.

"The storage room looked like a bomb had hit it. Those samples didn't fly off the rolling racks and scatter all over the place on their own. A mess that huge means a life-or-death-level struggle took place. This wasn't your run-of-the-mill murder. It was a rage killing. A victim of rape is a prime candidate for revenge and to commit such a gruesome murder."

Sonia rubbed her chin. "You made a compelling case for Avril and the twins, but unless I missed something, there wasn't a trace of physical evidence at the scene of the crime to tie any of them to the murder. So, unless one of them confesses, it is impossible to prove any of them is the killer."

Joan smirked, "So, Miss Marple, which is more effective: a rubber hose or a baseball bat to beat a confession out of one of them?"

Chapter Thirty

We finally had a lull in the action. I took a potty break and, since I was already out, I walked a few aisles over to Avril Wilts' booth. I stopped one door before Avril's booth and peered in. If she had a roomful of customers, I'd come back later.

Avril was alone, so I strolled into her booth as if I owned the place. I plastered an insincere smile on my kisser and stood across from her at a worktable. "If I were the suspicious type, I'd swear you've been avoiding me."

She looked up from an order pad with surprise. "Why would I avoid you?"

I rolled my eyes. "Don't play dumb, Avril. It's beneath you. You knew damn well I'd be in your face about you and the Larsens lying to the police about Mariel." I smirked. "Classy people, those Larsens. They rushed out of town before the end of the market, leaving you holding the bag."

She jutted her jaw. "Nobody's holding the bag, and nobody's lying, and you can't prove any different, or the police would have arrested us for perjury by now."

"My mother was there and said you're lying."

"Not the entire time. She went to the powder room."

I nodded. "True. And Mariel was holding the coconut when my mother went to the powder room. Mariel wasn't holding the coconut when my mother returned. So, unless Mariel shoved it down her pants, the only explanation is that while my mother was in the powder room, Mariel threw the coconut into the trash container in the theater lobby the way she told the police."

Avril pursed her lips. "Or your mother's the one lying to protect her boss."

I tsked. "Smooth move. So, you think that the best way to get an order from my mother is to question her integrity."

She shrugged. "You can't lose what you're never going to get."

I framed my hands like a movie director. "Either you're vindictive enough to lie and get an innocent woman arrested for a crime she couldn't commit as payback for her not writing you any orders, or you framed her by lying to the police because you are Simon's killer."

Avril slammed the order pad on the worktable. "This insulting conversation is *over*." She spoke through clenched teeth. "Get out of my booth, or I'll call security and have you removed."

I held out my hands in supplication. "No problem. I've said everything I came to say, and I'm leaving." I favored her with an extra-strong shot of my famous death ray glare. "But before I go, consider this: Unless Mariel Levine stood on stilts, she wasn't tall enough to reach the back of Simon's head and impale him." I formed my fingers into a pistol and aimed it at her head. "*You, on the other hand, are the perfect height.* Detective Lehrman isn't a stupid man. He'll figure it out, and I promise, *he'll be looking for you.*"

As I turned the corner to go back to our aisle, Walter Seiden fell in step with me.

He arched a brow. "This might come as a surprise, but subtlety may not be your best asset."

I grinned. "Bless the Goddess for small favors."

He dipped his head. "Trolling for a reaction, or you've got information the rest of us don't?"

"A little bit of both."

"Such as?"

"Unless she stood on stilts, a woman standing only five feet four couldn't impale the tip of a coconut shell into the brain stem of a six feet two inches tall man."

"Mariel's short stature wasn't an issue for your detective friend to arrest her."

"You're right. In his rush to close it, he stupidly based his *entire case* on Avril and her boss's disputing Mariel's alibi. Facts and science are stubborn things. The impact of Mariel's height on her inability to *physically commit the crime* is an indisputable fact."

Walter held up an index finger. "If Simon wasn't standing as the blow was struck, Mariel's height is immaterial."

I shook my head. "There was nothing to sit on in the storage room. Mariel is a short, slight, middle-aged woman who isn't strong enough to push Simon down to the ground, flip him onto his stomach, and keep him down with Simon thrashing about long enough to shove the tip of the coconut into his brain stem. Mark my words. Avril's motive for committing perjury will be her undoing."

"Why are you so sure Avril is the killer?" He pointed to himself. "She isn't the only tall one. If you're using height as the smoking gun, you should consider Lucinda, her sister, and me as candidates too."

I nodded. "You all meet the height requirement, but Avril is the *only one* who had issues with *both* Simon and Mariel. And there are only two reasons for her to lie to the police. Either Avril is vindictive enough to lie and get an innocent woman arrested for a crime she was physically incapable of committing, or Avril framed Mariel by lying to the police because she killed Simon."

Chapter Thirty-One

My internal alarm clock rang an hour early the next morning. Since going back to sleep wasn't an option, I pulled on my shorts and a tank top, laced up my sneakers, and headed out for a walk on the beach. The sun fought a losing battle trying to break through an overcast sky, the dark gray color of wet cement that hung over the roiling, murky Atlantic. The anxious ocean matched my nervous anticipation of the arrival of a storm of a different kind.

That early in the morning, the boardwalk was all mine, and I reached the pier in fifteen minutes. It was only half a dozen fishermen and me. I sat on a wooden bench facing east, watching the fishermen casting and recasting their lines. I inhaled a huge gulp of the briny salt air to cleanse yesterday's nasty Avril encounter out of my system. But with Simon's killer still at large, there was a fat chance of that happening.

Avril's response to my accusations was what I expected. But Walter's comments? Curious, to say the least. He challenged my reasons for Avril as the killer. That he shone the light of suspicion on himself, and the twins got my attention. Logic says he'd be all over my Avril theory like white to rice. It begged the question of why his response was the reverse.

I stared out into the horizon as dawn broke, but if the ocean held any answers, it wasn't in a sharing mood. Huge black clouds boiled over the fussy Atlantic as high tide brought close sets of waves crashing to the shoreline. It was time to boogie if I were to outrun the coming storm. Before the clouds burst, I stepped up my pace back to the hotel.

As the hotel came into view, a deep male voice from behind me yelled, "*Look out on your left!*" Instinct took over, and I jumped to the right as far as possible, but not quickly enough to avoid the handlebars of a ten-speed touring bike. Momentum slammed me into the metal handrail of the boardwalk wall.

The bastard never even slowed down, let alone stopped to see if I was injured. I tried to yell at the jerk, but the best my chest produced was a weak squeak like a wheezing mouse who had a bad case of emphysema.

A fisherman in his late sixties with thinning, grayish-yellow hair was the man who yelled the warning. He cupped his weathered hands around his mouth to form a megaphone and yelled at the top of his lungs. "*Hey, you! Hotshot on the ten-speed! Stop*!" But by then, the bike and its miscreant rider were mere stick figures in the distance.

The fisherman glared at the biker's receding outline. "Damned bikers. Why the hell aren't they required to pass a driver's test and be licensed? The law is clear: A bicyclist riding on sidewalks or in crosswalks must yield the right-of-way to pedestrians and must give an audible signal before passing." He pointed to the boardwalk. "This is the same as a sidewalk. If the infraction occurred in front of a cop, the bicyclist would have been ticketed and arrested for leaving the scene of an accident."

I nodded. "I'm from Los Angeles, and not only does the pedestrian *always* have the right of way, but it is against the law to ride a bike on the sidewalk. Bikers are only permitted to ride on the streets and in the bike lanes."

He touched his abdomen. "Can you take a deep breath? If not, it means you broke some ribs."

I shook my head. "I was only winded, but after smashing into that guardrail, I'll be black and blue from my armpits to my abdomen."

He asked, "Do you live far? I suggest you not drive. Do you have someone to come and get you? If you don't have anyone, I'll be glad to give you a lift." He smiled. "But if you're hinky getting into a car with a perfect stranger, I understand. No problem. I'll hail you a cab."

I motioned to the hotel. "I'm in town on business and staying at the hotel. I can get to the hotel and up to my room."

He said, "A doctor should examine you. Ask the hotel to send its house physician to your room. I'll walk you to the hotel and into the lobby." He took his ball cap off and waved it like Sir Walter Raleigh's cape. "Jimbo Johanssen at your service, Miss...?"

I blushed. "Please excuse my rudeness. My nana would be horrified. I'm Holly Schlivnik. Mr. Johanssen, I appreciate the offer, but it's not necessary."

He held out his hands. "Nonsense. I insist. My Meemaw raised me right. And please call me Jimbo. Mr. Johanssen was my daddy."

Chapter Thirty-Two

All things considered, I was damned lucky. I was ambulatory, and my injuries were minor—no broken bones; just some aches and pain that a few aspirins would cure. But the only way Jimbo Johanssen would let me get on with the rest of my day was if the hotel manager summoned the doctor. I bit my tongue not to laugh as Jimbo insisted on waiting until the house doctor arrived. I'd draw the line at his being in the examination room. LOL.

Twenty minutes later, a middle-aged guy dressed in tennis whites, carrying a black medical bag, strode purposefully into the hotel lobby and looked around. I flagged the doctor down and turned to my guardian angel. "Jimbo, thank you for all the help and concern. The doctor arrived, so your work is done. I promise to follow all the instructions the doctor gives me." I arched a brow. "I'd swear my overprotective father, who's out of the country right now, sent you to watch over me."

Jimbo winked mischievously. "Well, young lady, fathers are overprotective, especially of their daughters—so, perhaps..." He gave a two-fingered salute and scurried out the door.

Despite a time-consuming, but thorough examination, an awkward shower, as well as a challenge getting my undies on, I was only fifteen minutes late for breakfast. I eased my tush into a seat at the Yenta table and took several restorative sips of coffee. Once sufficiently caffeinated, I shared the latest Holly Swimsuit misadventure with the girls.

Hope lightly grazed my right wrist. "It's amazing you weren't more seriously hurt. Why aren't you in your room resting?" She pointed around the table. "We can handle the booth."

I shook my head. "The doctor said moving around is better than sitting or lying down. I'd be less stiff and heal sooner, being mobile. Besides, I'd go nuts in my room all day."

Sonia asked, "Did you recognize the biker?"

I shook my head. "No. It happened fast, and the only thing I focused on was whether I was seriously hurt. All I remember is the biker was tall."

Hope asked, "How could you tell their height if the rider was sitting?"

"By the seat. It was raised to the highest position."

Queenie asked, "Was the biker a man or a woman?"

I shrugged. "No clue. The rider wore a bike helmet, and their upper body was hunched over the handlebars, so it was impossible to tell. Since I didn't know the rider, it doesn't make any difference."

Joan bit her lip. "But maybe you did."

I clucked my tongue. "Joanie, this was a random accident caused by a careless biker."

Joan narrowed her eyes. "Was it? Why are you so sure?"

"What are you suggesting?"

"What if the biker was the killer, warning you to back off?"

I tsked. "Oh, come on. How could the killer know where I'd be on that exact day and time?"

Sonia said, "Someone with access to you, say Avril or Lucinda as an example, could plant a tracking device in your wallet or messenger bag."

I laughed out loud. "You guys watch too many TV cop shows. If *the killer* knocked me down, they'd make sure I didn't get up. Besides, even if she wanted to, Lucinda is in no shape to pull off such a stunt. But for giggles and squeaks, I'll ask Avril if she's a bike rider."

The concept of the biker being the killer was ludicrous. But I couldn't get the possibility out of my mind. So, I strolled into Avril's booth as though the altercation of the day before had never happened.

"Hey, Avril, how ya doin'?"

She eyed me with less enthusiasm than an infected tooth extraction. "Returning to fling more insults?"

Yeah. And who told you?

"Nah. Just wondering where you were this morning before dawn."

She checked her watch. "Happy hour doesn't begin until four o'clock in most establishments. But by asking such a ridiculously crazy question, it appears that you got a head start."

"So, where were you?"

"Seriously?"

"As a heart attack."

"Why?"

"Answer the question."

"*Where the hell do you think I was*?"

I smiled sweetly. "That's what I'm trying to find out."

She clucked her tongue. "Not that it's any of your business, but I was in bed asleep, the same as *most normal people*. Why?"

I ignored her question and answered with another of my own. "Do you ride a ten-speed touring bike?"

She burst out laughing. "Are you on medication?"

Yeah. And who told you?

"Do vitamins count?"

"Not unless yours are laced with a hallucinogen."

"So, do you ride a ten-speed touring bike or not?"

She rolled her eyes. "The answer is no. I don't ride a touring bike, a training bike, a motorbike, a mountain bike, or any other type of bike. I never learned to ride a bicycle. Now, tell me the reason why you care."

"Because I was walking northbound on the boardwalk, on the way back to my hotel from the pier right before sunup. A rider on a lightweight ten-speed touring bike rode too close and clipped me with their handlebars. The momentum threw me into the steel arm rail of the boardwalk wall." I pointed to my midsection. "Two sore ribs and I'm black and blue around my middle, and the bastard never even stopped."

She pinched her lips. "Let me assure you, if it were me on the bike, you wouldn't still be standing here, able to ask the question." She pointed to the booth entrance. "Since we've cleared this issue up, get the hell out of my booth and don't come back."

I blew her a kiss and got out while the getting was still good.

That went well—if your idea of a great time is a migraine. I doubt if I'll be invited to her house for Thanksgiving dinner. But at least Avril gave me an answer that confirmed my original theory that the bike incident was a random one committed by a stranger and not planned by someone I knew. Do I believe her? Yeah. Even an Academy Award-winning actor couldn't fake that level of righteous indignation. Was I disappointed or relieved? Maybe a little bit of both.

I texted Queenie that I had finished interrogating Avril and was making a detour to the food court for a chocolate chip cookie and coffee to celebrate that no blood had been shed during the questioning. I signed off with a promise to bring dessert and headed for Katie's Kookies, Kakes, N' Koffee. Ten minutes later, I precariously balanced a box filled with an assortment of mouth-watering cookies and a cardboard tray holding six to-go cups of piping-hot coffee.

Halfway across the food court, Walter Seiden appeared by my side.

I raised an eyebrow. "Walter, if I were the suspicious sort, I'd swear you planted a tracking device in my wallet. It seems no matter where I am, you magically appear."

He shrugged. "Just lucky, I guess."

I asked, "Are you coming or going?"

"I'm on the fence."

Huh?

"Walter, that's like being a little pregnant. Either you're arriving, or you're leaving. Which is it?"

"Arriving, but I hate eating alone." He lifted a grease-stained bag. "Any chance of convincing you to sit with me while I gobble down a burger and fries? An unexpected rush of accounts made me miss lunch."

I made a snap decision and hoped it was the right one. "Sure. We've got a microwave in the booth to reheat the coffee."

Chapter Thirty-Three

We sat across from one another at a table for four in the back quadrant of the food court. Walter polished off the burger and fries in a dozen healthy bites and washed it all down with a couple of swigs of lemonade out of a bottle. He patted his tummy. "As my youngest used to say as a toddler, *more better*."

"How many children do you have?"

He held up three fingers. "The two oldest are girls, and the baby is a boy, each three years apart. The eldest is twenty-four and the youngest eighteen."

"There are three children in our family, too, and the same gender breakdown as yours: two girls and a boy. I'm the oldest."

I asked, "Your wife worked or was she a stay-at-home mom?"

"She worked. She earned a PhD. in Chemical Engineering from Florida Institute of Technology. She was a researcher at a lab until she became ill."

"Did you go to college, too?"

He nodded. "FIT. We met at school."

"What was your field of study?"

"I earned a PhD. in Electrical Engineering."

As they say in the south: Well, shut mah mouth.

"*Why in the world are you selling swimsuits*?"

He held out his hands. "Electrical engineering companies are few and far between. The one I worked for merged with a larger firm, and the new parent company only wanted our accounts, not our employees. With two kids in college, my wife's income alone was not enough to pay for two tuitions and still make ends meet. I interviewed at half a dozen companies, but after six months, I didn't get a single offer, not even a lousy one to turn down. My mother's kid brother, Eddy, was the sales manager of Elegance Beach Accessories. Mom twisted his arm, and Eddy hired me as a rep. He gave me a crash course on selling cover-ups and sent me on the road. A year later, I picked up Mystique Swimwear and was doing great—until my wife became ill and had to stop working. We lost her income and health insurance."

He pinched his lips. "Then Simon Posnick convinced the Mystique management that with a sick wife, I'd quit traveling. Without even checking Posnick's story out, they yanked the line from me and gave it to him. I still had Elegance Beach Accessories, but the volume wasn't enough to pay the bills on its own. I needed to replace Mystique, but the season was half over, and there weren't any swimwear lines available. We went through every dime we'd saved for the kids' college and used it all for medical expenses. Every cent I earned went to my wife's medical expenses, too. My girls had to drop out of school. We lost our house to foreclosure two months before the holidays and had to move in with my in-laws. It's taken me two years to claw my way out of the financial pit we'd fallen into."

I dipped my head. "How can you possibly go back to Mystique now, considering the horrible way they treated you?"

He shrugged. "When I lost Mystique, my uncle gave me great advice: Don't get mad, get even."

Get even with whom?

"How?"

"By writing so much business for them that I'd become indispensable."

Walter blushed, and all of a sudden, he found something fascinating on the ceiling. "Uh, remember we talked about having dinner?"

I nodded.

He smiled sadly. "I promised my wife I wouldn't live the rest of my life alone. I thought—well, I was ready and hoped you'd be interested in me that way. But since you're not, uh, well, the thing is, I considered your comment, and I'm okay with us going out as friends for now. Down the road, maybe things could change for us..."

I shook my head. "Walter, it only works that way in movies and romance novels, not in real life. Besides, I live across the country in LA. Long-distance romances rarely work out, and I'm not interested in having one. But even if I was, you might think you're ready to move on, but trust me, you're not."

His tone turned huffy. "What makes you such an expert in grief and going on with your life?"

I surreptitiously looked around for my two favorite ghosts, expecting them to whirl next to me. I was half-relieved and half-disappointed when they failed to appear.

"I've been in a relationship with a widower for over a year. Let me tell you, nothing is worse than playing second fiddle to the ghost of a man's dead wife." I pointed to Walter's wedding band. "Buddy also still wears his wedding band. And worse, not a day goes by that he doesn't refer to her. Marie is so much a part of my relationship with Buddy, it's the same as being in a threesome."

Walter's eyes filled as he whispered, "I have no idea how to move on."

I covered my hand over his, and he flinched. "When the time is right for you to move on, you will. Or, you might never be ready. Either way, it'll be the right thing for you."

Walter brightened, "Not to be nosy, but it was impossible not to overhear your round two with Avril." He grinned elfishly. "Did I hear right? You asked her what she was doing this morning before dawn?"

I nodded. "Yeah. Some idiotic bike rider almost mowed me down on the boardwalk at sunrise and never stopped to see if I was okay."

"And you suspected *Avril Wilts* was the biker?"

"After yesterday's soirée, you betcha. I wouldn't put anything past her."

"How could she know where you were at a particular time?" His tone was incredulous. "*You think she's stalking you*?"

I shrugged. "I mentioned in the course of a conversation that I walk daily from the hotel to the pier and back on the boardwalk at the crack of dawn."

"You still think it was her?"

"As the biker? I'm inclined to believe she never learned to ride a bicycle. As to her being Simon's killer, nothing changed my mind to the contrary."

Walter screwed up his nose as if he'd taken a whiff of rotten vegetables. "What kind of parents don't teach their kids how to ride a bike? First of all, by learning to ride a bike, kids become independent. They can get around on their own and don't always have to depend on their parents to cart them from place to place. Secondly, it teaches kids responsibility—to take good care of their bike, remember to lock it properly, learn and obey traffic laws, and always wear protective gear. And last but not least, it's a great family activity. Before Sarah became ill, each Sunday morning, the five of us biked six miles to the Nibble N' Nosh Deli at South Beach for breakfast. Sometimes we made a day of it at the beach. Other times, it was only breakfast and a round trip. But either way, it was something we all looked forward to doing together."

Walter sighed. "If Avril experienced a family activity like biking as a kid, she might have a more agreeable disposition as an adult."

"I'm..." My sentence was interrupted by the ring of my cell phone. I glanced at the Caller ID and my heart rate ramped up to warp speed: *Lois Lowenstein, Esq*.

I turned to Walter. "Please excuse me. I've gotta take this call."

Chapter Thirty-Four

The next morning, I wasn't ready to run a marathon, but I could bend over to pull my undies on and not see stars. Okay, okay, stop laughing. You're wondering, *the last time Schlivnik ran a marathon was...?* The second Tuesday of last week. Fine. Be that way.

But to my credit, for once in my life, I chose not to push the envelope and skipped the pre-dawn walk. I stopped at the hotel lobby kiosk on my way to the Brews N' Bagels and bought a copy of the *East Coast Apparel News*.

Ten minutes later, I slid into my seat at the Yenta table and, between bites of a bagel and sips of strong coffee, I recapped yesterday's events. I spread the newspaper across the center. The double headline above the fold read:

Bikini Buyer Beats Bust

Coconut Killer at Large

Joan peered over the top of her eyeglasses. "So, Miss Marple, since Mariel was sprung from the hoosegow, did you ID Simon's killer yet, or are you still considering other suspects?"

I said, "I am still considering other suspects, but I now sympathize with Siggie chasing his tail."

Sonia dipped her head. "Meaning?"

"Meaning, Walter brought up that he and his family biked on Sundays before his wife got sick, and that confused me."

Hope asked, "How?"

I held out my hands. "One minute he looked innocent because he brought it up, and the next minute, he looked guilty and was doing an in plain sight stunt to fake me out."

Queenie tapped the tip of her nose. "Neither scenario makes any sense for any of the suspects. Not one of them would know where you'd be at any given time."

Hope said, "Check your messenger bag and wallet for any bugs or tracking devices."

I rolled my eyes.

Sonia asked, "So, you believe Avril wasn't the biker, but do the twins ride bikes?"

I shrugged. "I haven't confronted the twins yet. But even if she does ride, Lucinda is in no shape to pedal anywhere."

Queenie asked, "Have you uncovered any physical evidence tying any of the suspects to the crime scene?"

Yes, tons. And I'm keeping it all a state secret.

But to play nice in the sandbox, I kept the snarky comment to myself. "Not yet. But I am still convinced Avril is the killer."

Joan picked up her bagel and poked her index finger through the center. "Without any proof, you've got the hole from the bagel for your trouble."

Sonia rubbed her chin. "And since you're now persona non grata at Avril's booth, your chances of finding any physical evidence tying her to the murder went from slimsky to nonesky."

Nothing gets past this crew.

Hope patted my arm. "Hol, even the police, with all their resources, can't solve every murder, and neither can you. Some killers do get away with murder. This might be one of those times. My advice? Throw in the towel and move on. You gave it your best shot."

The smart money said Hope's analysis was spot on.

But nobody ever confused me with Albert Einstein.

The rest of the day, I had a bad case of *Shpilkes*, roughly translated as Yiddish for ants in my pants, so every hour or so, I took a stroll down

Avril's aisle. Was I expecting a smoking gun to pop out of her booth and say howdy? Yep. Regrettably, I had no such luck. All I accomplished was being on the receiving end of Avril's death ray glare. The only good thing? Walter was too busy working with customers all day to ask me out on another date.

My mother called after lunch to invite me to a celebration dinner with Mariel, her family, and Lo-Lo. When I told the girls that I would be leaving early to prepare for the party, the Yentas practically pushed me out of the booth. Go figure.

I went back to my hotel room to shower and change for the party. While I couldn't imagine it possible, Hope's comment that my wallet and messenger bag could be bugged stuck in my head. I emptied my wallet and messenger bag and thoroughly examined their contents. As expected, all items were in their rightful place. Nothing odd. No bugs—neither the electronic nor creepy crawly type. An annoying combination of relief and disappointment twisted my innards as I put everything back.

Chapter Thirty-Five

Midnight, the next morning

As she made the transition onto I-95 south, Mom said, "In all the years we've lived in Miami, I've never seen I-95 this empty."

I said, "Do you often drive from Lauderhill to your home at midnight?"

"No. This is a first. It was always with your dad, and he drove."

I giggled. "Let me guess. You fell asleep in the car, right?"

"Right. How did you know?"

"Because if I'm a passenger in a car, I do the same thing. Genetics is odd, isn't it? I inherited that from you, and Nana's nervous habit of laughing when she found out that someone had died."

Mom tsked. "At least you also inherited her love of jewelry and perfume."

I covered my mouth to stifle a yawn. "Mariel Levine certainly can party-hardy."

"Not many things warrant a party-hardy more than having first-degree murder charges against you dropped."

I asked, "Were you surprised that she played the steel drum?"

Mom laughed. "Quite. And for how well she danced Reggae. The Calypso Café seemed an odd choice of venues, and odder that she pre-ordered the meal."

I said, "Well, she certainly ordered wonderful dishes. Everything was delicious—from the Jerk Chicken to the sweet potato pudding, to the coco bread. The Jamaican hot pepper shrimp almost set my mouth on fire. Once Mariel suggested taking a drink of my frozen Bob Marley to cool it down, I enjoyed the shrimp dish. How did Mariel become such an expert on Jamaica?"

"It turns out that Murray and Mariel lived in Lauderhill when they first got married. The Levines lived across the street from Everton and Raeni Campbell, the owners of the Calypso Café. Mariel and Murray frequented the café and learned about Jamaican culture from the Campbells."

I said, "Mariel's speech appreciating the gift of freedom and all the support she received from family, friends, and the industry was so moving. But when she called me out and asked me to come up to the head table, and thanked me in front of all the guests, it was surprising and embarrassing. And she said I had a thank-you gift on the way? Why? I only did what any decent person would have done."

Mom asked, "Why were you surprised, let alone embarrassed? Mariel was right when she said you saved her bacon. You arranged for a top-notch criminal attorney to represent her. It was the information you gave to Dr. Jones that proved it was physically impossible for Mariel to kill Mr. Posnick. That information was instrumental in the charges being dropped and Mariel's release. Don't sell yourself short, Hol. If it wasn't for you as her greatest advocate, Mariel Levine might have spent the rest of her life in prison."

"I owe my career to two people: Dad and Mariel Levine. She was there for me. Now, it's my turn to support her."

Mom said, "I'm proud of you, kiddo. You done good."

I rubbed my hands together. "Do you have any idea what the gift is?"

"Nope. She never consulted me, so I've no clue."

"I guess I'll find out soon enough." I laughed. "Hopefully, the mystery gift arrives before I go back to LA."

Mom cleared her throat, and her tone of voice turned serious. "I-I want to talk to you."

Panic squeezed my heart.

Dear Goddess, please don't let my mother be ill.

Don't jump to any conclusions.

Yeah, right.

I struggled to keep the quiver out of my voice.

"Okay, sure."

"This nightmare of Mariel's arrest and my having to step in and take over for her while she was in jail made me reflect seriously on my life and the direction I want for my future."

Whew. That's all? No problem.

"So, what conclusions have you come to?"

"Now that Dad has retired, my life is going to change, too." Her tone of voice turned guilty, like a kid caught with her hand in the cookie jar. "Don't take this the wrong way, but the idea of him being underfoot twenty-four hours a day is enough to send me over the edge."

Duh. Better you than me, Mom.

I chirped my reply with the enthusiasm of a robin welcoming spring. "No worries. You work during the week, so the issue will only be on weekends. Besides, his retired buddies will keep him busy. Between their card games, backgammon, golf, and season tickets to professional sports events, he'll be occupied most of the time."

Mom sighed. "The thing is, I want to keep working, but not full-time. That way, I can spend *some time* with Dad too."

"So, what's your plan?"

"I love Mariel and my job, but I'm going to look around for something with flexible hours and only three days a week."

"Did you discuss this with Mariel? You're such an integral part of her business, she'd hate to lose you."

"I'm sure she'd try to accommodate me, but reduced, flexible hours are not feasible for fast-paced, time-sensitive fashion operations. I can't expect Mariel to wait until I'm in the office to get something done."

"You're in a great spot right now: a boss you enjoy working for and a job you like doing. Are you sure you want to give it up?"

Mom said, "I am."

I said, "I've got an idea, but I'm not ready to discuss it yet. Give me a day or two to work out the details, and I'll come back to see if it's to your liking."

Five minutes later, Mom pulled into the main entrance of the hotel and stopped at the front door. She leaned over and grazed her lips across my forehead. "Always remember, I love you a bushel and a peck and a hug around the neck."

An unexpected lump formed in my throat as my mother recited part of the childhood song she sang to us kids nightly when she put us to bed.

I squeezed her hand and got out of the car. I waited until she drove out of the parking lot and onto Collins Avenue before I went into the hotel lobby.

I waved to Abigail, the night manager. I was halfway to the elevator bank when she called me back. "Ms. Schlivnik, excuse me, please come back. A package arrived for you. Let me go into the storage room and get it. I won't be but a minute or two."

Strange. If this is Mariel's gift, why not give it to me at the party? She made a point of apologizing that she had something for me, but it didn't arrive in time for the party.

Abigail lifted a beautifully wrapped box onto the registration desk and winked. "Somebody did something right..."

I pulled the box closer and looked it over. "Abigail, please check in the back to see if the card fell off."

"I checked the rack and the floor of the storage room before bringing it out. There was no card." She smiled. "How lovely to receive a gift from a secret admirer."

I said, "Or the sender put the card inside the box. Did you happen to notice the delivery person?"

She dipped her head. "Sorry, I came on duty at eleven o'clock, and the package was already in the storage room."

"Do you keep a log sheet to check in package deliveries?"

"Yes, a package is logged when it is delivered by a carrier. We keep separate logs for each carrier. Since a carrier didn't deliver the package, it had no paperwork or any information to enter into a log." She pointed to a slip of paper with my name and room number handwritten on it and taped to the top right corner of the box. "Whoever accepted the package put this on it to identify the recipient."

"So, how do you find out who accepted it or the time of day it arrived?"

Abigail held out her hands. "At the shift change, I'll leave a note to ask whoever accepted it to please contact you."

I put my ear to the box and joked. "At least it's not ticking."

Abigail laughed. "Thank goodness for small favors! Hopefully, the card is inside the box, so you'll know who to thank for their thoughtfulness. If not, you've got a secret admirer."

Chapter Thirty-Six

Thirty minutes later, there wasn't a square inch of free space in the place once Moisés Lehrman, two MBPD uniformed officers, and a three-member crime scene team stormed into my hotel room.

Normally put together as neat as a pin, Mo's clothes were rumpled, and his wavy brown hair stood on end, as if he'd stuck a finger into an electric socket. Anyone could tell I'd woken him from a deep sleep, and that he'd thrown on yesterday's clothes.

Mo strode across the room and folded me into his strong arms. His voice caught as he talked into my hair. "Thank you for calling me."

He led me to a small table and chairs next to the window facing the ocean and motioned for me to sit. "Let me get my team organized, and then I'll be back to talk to you."

He turned to the older of the two uniforms. "Sergeant Riley, go downstairs to the lobby. Ask the night manager to provide you with a computer printout with the names and contact information of all the employees on duty for the last twenty-four hours. Next, interview all the employees on duty now. It's doubtful they'll be any help since the night manager said the package was already in the storage room before the shift change at eleven o'clock. But at least we can eliminate those employees. Focus on the employees on duty for the first two shifts."

Riley gave Mo a two-fingered salute and went out the door.

Mo faced the younger officer. "Officer Perez, secure the downstairs perimeter. Block off the storage room with crime scene tape, as well as any additional areas where the package was. Ask the night manager to explain the process for receiving a package like the one for Ms. Schlivnik. Then, establish a timeline." Perez nodded and left.

Then, Mo turned his attention to a middle-aged Asian woman. He pointed to the open box on the makeup table. "Sergeant Yieh, the bloody coconut shell and threatening letter are inside the box. Have your team process the box and its contents. Dust the box, its contents, and the wrapping paper for fingerprints. Then go down to the lobby and dust the storage room. Focus on the shelf where the package was."

Sergeant Yieh nodded, grabbed her fingerprint kit, and joined her crew.

Mo sat across from me and looked me in the eye. "Tell me *everything*. Leave nothing out. Not a single detail, big or small, because you think it's not important or relevant. Let me be the judge of that."

So, I did. For an hour and a half.

He took no notes. His cheek bunched a couple of times, but he listened intently, without interrupting, and asked no questions.

Hoarse and all talked out at the end, I braced myself for his retribution.

He covered his hand over mine. "I'm so sorry I couldn't prevent something this awful from happening to you. I promise I won't rest until the sender is captured."

My reaction?

I almost fell out of my chair.

"That's it? No lectures? No threat of jail?"

He shrugged. "What would be the point when calling you out would only strengthen your resolve?"

I rolled my eyes. "Cut the crap, Detective. You can't admit that I told you so. You climbed up the wrong tree. Let me offer you a piece of humble pie with your next cup of coffee."

He grinned. "Mea culpa."

I asked, "So, what happens now?"

"We wait for the test results. If we get lucky, Avril Wilts was sloppy, and her fingerprints are all over the box."

"And if there are no prints on it?"

He smiled evilly. "No place does it say we're required to share the information."

Chapter Thirty-Seven

The techs tried their best to clean up the grainy black fingerprint powder mess all over the room, but neatness took a back seat to thoroughness. So, despite their efforts, the place still looked as if a coal mine had exploded inside it. I made a mental note to leave a generous tip for housekeeping as an apology for the mess.

It was three a.m. when the uniforms and the crime scene team finally left. I wasn't in the mood for any company. But Mo insisted on staying, and I didn't have the energy to argue. We fell into bed fully dressed and wrapped in one another's arms, clinging tightly to one another as a life preserver, unwilling or unable to let go.

I awoke at dawn's first light and was in bed alone. A combination of relief and regret twisted my heart. Mo had tucked a scribbled note on his pillow to say he would be done interviewing the morning shift hotel employees around noon and would meet me at the Mermaid booth. He instructed that I wait for him and not interrogate Avril on my own. I crossed my fingers behind my back and mumbled my agreement.

I took a coolish shower to jolt myself into action. I was dressed and at our table at Brews N' Bagels at the usual time. I downed a full cup of java and advised the ladies to do the same before I began sharing my latest tale. Once adequately caffeinated, the Yentas sat open-mouthed as I recounted the activities of the night before.

Hope asked, "What did the threatening note say?"

I reached into my messenger bag and pulled out a mechanical pencil, and tore a blank sheet out of a notebook.

"The note was unsigned, and typed in jumbled upper and lower-case letters that looked something like these and said,

DoN'T STicK yOuR NosE WherE It DOesN'T BeLOnG
Or yOU wIlL ENd Up ThE SamE wAy aS sIMoN
mIND yOUr OwN BUsinEsS YoU HavE BEeN wARnEd

Joan bit her lower lip. "The note was unsigned, so why are you so sure Avril sent the package?"

Fear and exhaustion made me cranky and not in control of my tongue. "Who the hell else sent it?" I snickered. "Mariel Levine?"

Sonia pinched her brow. "Hol, in your heart of hearts, you *want it to be Avril*, but the reality is *any of the other suspects* could have sent it."

Queenie tapped her index finger to the tip of her nose. "The fingerprint tests will be the telling of the tale. Hopefully, Detective Lehrman will have received the results by the time he meets you at our booth."

Hope ran her fingers through the crown of her hair. "And if the fingerprint tests are inconclusive?"

I tapped a teaspoon rat-a-tat-tat on the edge of the table to make my point. "I'll put the Mike Schlivnik method to work. If the front door is locked, go through the back door. If the back is shut, go through the window. Persistence counts. Ask enough questions and dig deep enough, and the truth will always come out."

As promised, Mo arrived at our booth at noon. We took the long way around to Avril's aisle so he could bring me up to speed.

He grinned. "I'm shocked. I fully expected you to have confronted our suspect already"

I cuffed his chin. "You arrived just in the nick of time."

He rolled his eyes. "Thank goodness there was no traffic."

"So, Columbo, are you any smarter today?"

He grimaced. "Regrettably, no. I brought two uniforms with me this morning. Between the three of us, we interviewed the entire hotel staff on duty the morning before. And not one of them, including the desk clerk who wrote the note with your name and room number attached to the outside of the box, remembered a single thing about the delivery person. I instructed the two officers to return to the hotel for the next shift change and interview everyone on duty."

"Any word on the fingerprints?"

"Three sets were on the outside of the package, and one set was on the coconut and the threatening letter. Sergeant Yieh ran the prints through the statewide system, but there were no matches."

I said, "So, one set is the suspect's, one set is the delivery person's, and the third one is the hotel clerk's. So, since there was no match, none of them has been in trouble with the law."

I bit my lower lip. "How about taking a different approach in questioning Avril?"

"Such as?"

"Don't accuse her of anything. Instead, say that you're interested in eliminating her as a suspect. Ask her to pick up a piece of paper and tell her we need her fingerprints to clear her."

"A bit underhanded, but it might work." Mo grinned. "If you ever get tired of hawking bikinis, you've got a great future as a detective."

I laughed out loud. "Surely you jest. Considering my inability to obey orders, I wouldn't last a day."

Mo dipped his head. "You got me there."

We turned the corner to Avril's aisle, and my heart sank to my toes. Her booth was dark and locked up tight as a drum.

Walter noticed us and walked to the entrance of his booth. "Are you just strolling the aisles, or are you on police business?"

I smiled. "A little bit of both." I pointed to Avril's booth. "We hoped to chat with Avril. Have you seen her today?"

Walter nodded. "She was in her booth earlier, but she ran out in a big rush and hasn't been back."

Mo asked, "How long ago?"

Walter tapped his lip. "Around an hour after I opened up my booth."

I asked, "Did she mention where she was going?"

Walter shook his head. "I was working with an account, and only noticed Avril leave out of the corner of my eye. I'm sorry I can't be more helpful. But when she comes back, I'll tell her you were looking for her."

"Thanks, Walter. Tell her to come to my booth."

We walked to the end of the aisle, and I said, "This adventure has been a big goose egg, so far. Hopefully, Avril comes back soon, and Walter remembers to give her the message."

Mo glanced at his watch. "I'd wait around and see, but I need to get back to the hotel and check how the shift change interviews are going. If she comes back, text me, and I'll come right over. If you're free for dinner tonight, I'll hang around the hotel and wait for you or pick you up at the convention center if it's better for you."

I dipped my head. "Gee, I'm sorry, but I'm busy tonight. Queenie, Harriet, and I are having dinner together and then a post-mortem season planning meeting afterwards. I'll have to take a rain check."

"Okay, check your calendar for the next couple of nights."

Mo's stomach growled, and I laughed out loud.

He blushed. "I haven't eaten anything since dinner last night. Did you have lunch yet?"

I shook my head. "No. We had a steady stream of customers all morning, and then you arrived."

He asked, "Do you have time for a bite?"

I nodded. "The booth is covered. They won't need me." I hooked my arm into the crook of his elbow. "The food court is down this corridor. I'll text Queenie to let her know we're stopping for lunch and ask if anyone wants me to bring something back."

Chapter Thirty-Eight

We weren't jammed, but we worked with a steady stream of accounts for the rest of the day. So, I didn't have any time to go back to Avril's booth, nor did she contact me. Big shock. Not. Either Walter didn't give her my message, or she chose to ignore it. I texted Mo to update him, and he texted back that the afternoon shift of hotel employees was as unhelpful as the other two groups. In terms of the investigation, the day was a big nothingburger all the way around.

We closed up for the night at six sharp. The Yentas walked back to the hotel, and Lauren went across the aisle to Lucinda's booth.

It was a toasty eighty-two degrees and ninety percent humidity when Harriet, Queenie, and I exited the convention center. Perspiration poured out of every bodily crevice in salty rivulets. Who knew toenails sweated?

Harriet mopped the sweat off her forehead with her wrist. "You ladies are not going to be happy. It was so crowded this morning that I either had to park on the street a mile away or in the back parking lot. I chose door number two and was lucky to nab the last open space. There is no sense in all of us roasting. Why don't you two wait inside the main building, and I'll text you when I am in front?"

Queenie and I looked at one another. "Nah. It'll be a lot faster to get out if you don't have to go completely around the entire convention center complex to get to the front."

Harriet nodded. "You're right. The reservation at Fabio's is at seven o'clock. The southbound I-95 will be brutal. And trust me, we don't want to be late. The food is to die for, and you don't have to sell a kidney to pay for the meal, so the place is always mobbed. The maître d' is a stickler for being on time. If you're five minutes late, he gives your table away, and your name goes to the bottom of the list."

I turned a visual one-eighty. No nosy neighbors. "Okay. But as long as we're on the way and nobody is around, I have something to discuss."

Harriet and Queenie nodded.

"Lucinda might not admit it, but I'd bet my boat that she was beaten and raped by Simon. And if he raped Lucinda, the twins had a helluva motive to kill him, and can't be eliminated as suspects. For all we know, the twins had every intention of killing Simon, but Avril beat them to the punch." I held out my hands in supplication. "While you can't be convicted in a court of law for your intentions, all the same... It breaks my heart to say it, but if Lauren lied about the attack, what else did she lie about? Her lying is a dealbreaker, as far as I am concerned."

Queenie asked, "So, what do you want to do?"

I shrugged. "Let her go."

I turned to Harriet. "That's my take, but you work with her full-time, so you're the one most impacted if we fire her. So, what say you?"

Harriet furrowed her brow. "On the one hand, she lied to protect her sister, not a customer. On the other hand, there would always be a cloud over her head regarding anything else."

Queenie asked, "If we let Lauren go now, how difficult will it be to replace her with someone as experienced?"

Harriet blew the air out through her cheeks. "*That's the big question*. All the experienced showroom managers are already working. Most of them have been with the same companies for years and would not be interested in making a change. Hiring a newbie and training them our way is an option. But training takes time, and in a seasonal business, it is crucial to hit the ground running. So, letting Lauren go without a replacement would be a big problem."

I asked, "Do you need someone five days a week?"

Harriet shook her head. "Not all the time."

I said, “If someone coming in three days a week works for you, I’ve got the perfect replacement.”

Queenie and Harriet chorused, “Who?”

I grinned. “My mother.”

Chapter Thirty-Nine

Fifteen minutes later, we reached the back of the convention center, where the loading dock faced the auxiliary parking lot. Only half a dozen cars were still scattered throughout the lot. Harriet's car was in the last row before the asphalt ended and the field where Lucinda's attack began.

It was dusk, and the parking lot was unlit, so we quickened our pace. The fastest way to get to Harriet's row was to cut across the lot on the diagonal. Harriet and Queenie were ten steps ahead of me. Their legs are longer than mine, and my shorter stride can never keep up with theirs.

The only car in the two rows before Harriet's was a nondescript blue four-door imported sedan. As I walked past it, I glanced inside the driver's side window. And stopped short. I pressed my face against the window for a closer look. Holy Guacamole. The driver was slumped over the steering wheel. I pulled on the door handle, but it was locked. I ran around to the other doors, but none of them opened either. I raced back to the driver's side. I banged on the window and yelled, "Are you okay?" No response. A second time. Zip. The third time wasn't a charm.

I cupped my hands around my mouth to form a megaphone and yelled at the top of my lungs, "*Hold up, girls. A person is slumped over the steering wheel in this blue car. It's impossible to tell if they're breathing. All four doors are locked, and the windows are up. Queenie, call nine-one-one. Harriet, open your trunk and bring the universal lug wrench so we can smash the window in.*"

Harriet ran to her car and opened the trunk. She turned around and yelled, "Where do I find it, and what's it look like?"

I sighed. "Never mind, it'll be faster to find it myself."

I ran to her car and removed the spare tire from the trunk.

I glared at Harriet. "You don't know how to change a flat tire?"

She wrinkled her forehead. "No. And you do?"

I rolled my eyes. "You bet your sweet ass I do. Mike Schlivnik forbade any of us kids from getting behind the wheel of a car until we proved we could. If your tire goes flat, then what?"

She made a fist and held it to her ear like a phone. "Call Auto Rescuers."

"And if you're in a place with no cellphone connectivity?"

"Wait for a good Samaritan to stop and help."

"And if no one stops?"

She shrugged.

I clucked my tongue. "It's hard to believe my dad let you go on the road not knowing how to change a tire."

She sniffed, "The subject never came up."

I said, "He assumed you could change a flat. Or that I taught you how."

Nana's voice whispered, "*The first three letters of assume are...*"

I reached into the wheel well and pulled out the lug wrench. I ran back to the blue car and smashed the heavy tool into the driver's side back window. The window was veined and cracked diagonally, but it took three swings before the glass shattered. I smacked the remaining glass shards out of the frame with the wrench head.

I covered my hand with my shirt sleeve and gingerly reached in and unlocked the door. I opened it and kicked the loose glass shards off the seat and onto the floor. I crawled into the back seat and climbed over the passenger's side of the front seat. I opened my messenger bag and pulled out my cell phone. I clicked on the flashlight and leaned over to get closer to the body. The front of the car was completely splattered with blood. I gagged as I recognized Avril Wilts' blood-drenched tiger print jumpsuit on the torso draped across the steering wheel.

Alert the media. For the first time in my sleuthing life, I didn't burst out laughing upon discovering a corpse.

I opened the front passenger door and stretched across the bench seat on my belly. Careful not to touch or move the body, I positioned my head between Avril's body and the seat to check if she was breathing. I didn't need an MD next to my name to make a diagnosis. Avril Wilts was as dead as it gets. A half-dollar-sized round hole in the lower part of the front of her neck was caused by a self-inflicted gunshot from the .38 Special Lady Smith hot pink-grip pistol clamped tightly in Avril Wilts' right hand. A copy of yesterday's *East Coast Apparel News* with the headline:

Bikini Buyer Beats Bust

Coconut Killer at Large

was next to a blood-splattered, typed note under Avril's right hand. I twisted my torso into a pretzel and read the note: "*I killed Simon Posnick. I can't live with the guilt. God forgive me.*"

Twenty minutes later, sirens shrieked a pulsing series of ear-splitting wails, and bubble lights blazed as Mo Lehrman, two patrol cars, the Miami-Dade Medical Examiner's wagon carrying Jazzy and her crew, a crime scene team, and an EMT crew all converged on the back parking lot of the convention center.

Mo parked his car and joined our trio. He pointed to the body slumped over the car's steering wheel. "Do you recognize the victim?"

I nodded. "Avril Wilts."

I grinned. "It turned out she had a good excuse for not being available to answer our questions."

His voice squeaked an incredulous two octaves higher. "*So, you went looking for her*?"

I rolled my eyes. "No. We were going to Harriet's car, and as I passed that blue four-door sedan, out of the corner of my eye, I noticed that a body was slumped over the steering wheel. I put my face against the window for a closer look. The steering wheel hid the person's face. I pounded on the driver's side window several times and yelled, asking if the person was okay. There was no response, so I used a universal lug wrench to smash the back driver's side rear window. I opened the back door and crawled over the front seat to check on her condition. I recognized the tiger print jumpsuit on the body and realized it was Avril Wilts.

"I opened the front passenger door and stretched across the seat on my belly to position my head under the body to check if she was breathing. That's when I discovered the gunshot neck wound and the pistol clamped in her right hand."

"Did you touch or move the body?"

I waved him off. "No. The only thing I did was call nine-one-one."

Mo gave me a thumbs-up and motioned for Jazzy to join us as she extricated herself from the passenger's front seat of Avril's car.

Mo pointed to Avril's body. "Can you confirm a TOD?"

Jazzy shrugged. "You know the drill. Nothing official until she's on the table and we get the toxicology and stomach contents test results back to determine the Post Mortem Interval."

I asked, "What's that?"

Jazzy said, "The time difference between the time of death and the body examination is called the Post Mortem Interval, or PMI. The longer the PMI, the larger the time the death window becomes, and the harder it will be to determine an accurate time of death. The body moves through four stages post death: pallor mortis, algor mortis, rigor mortis, and livor mortis. The vic has already gone through all the stages of death."

I said, "Please explain these stages in plain English, and not doctorese the way Snip does."

Jazzy laughed. "Absolutely. Pallor Mortis is the first stage and is the paleness in the face and other body parts, due to the cessation of blood circulation."

Jazzy held up her index and middle fingers. "Algor Mortis is the second stage. Within seconds of death, the brain cells begin to die, and the heart stops pumping blood. Without the brain and the blood distributing heat, the corpse eventually starts to match the outside temperature."

Jazzy waved her thumb, index, and middle fingers. "Rigor Mortis is the third stage. Immediately after death, all muscles become relaxed and limp. But the entire body will stiffen and become rigid after a few hours. Certain other deductions can be made based on the body's position in Rigor, such as whether the site the body was found is the site of death, if the person died in a particular position, etc. Expressions also freeze on the face of a victim, which helps in giving insight into the nature of their death. "

I asked, "What causes Rigor Mortis?"

Jazzy flexed her biceps. "Muscles require energy to function."

She waggled four fingers. "Livor Mortis is the final stage of death. Once the heart stops beating, the blood is at the mercy of gravity. Blood tends to collect in certain parts of the body, and it varies, depending on the body's position. After a few hours, the color changes from red to bluish-purple. This can take six to eight hours. After approximately twelve hours, the blood gets 'fixed' in place, and the skin does not turn white if pressed. The bluish coloring of the skin is called livor mortis or lividity. Lividity gives additional insight into the time of death and helps determine if the body was moved. All four of these stages of death often overlap. They usually start separately, but most of them continue simultaneously."

Mo asked, "So, if the vic went through all four stages of death, are you able to estimate the time of death?"

"Unofficially, between eight and twelve hours ago."

Chapter Forty

Needless to say, we never made it to our dinner reservation. By the time Mo took our statements and allowed us to leave, it was way past dinner time. It was just as well. Either the big, honkin' bullet hole in Avril's throat or Jazzy's descriptions of the four stages of death quashed our appetites. It could have gone either way.

We invited Harriet to join us for drinks, but she was probably the smartest one who begged off and went straight home. Queenie and I spent the remainder of the evening at the hotel bar, munching on beer nuts, polishing off a couple of bottles of Merlot, and trying unsuccessfully to make some sense of it all.

Thanks to the wine, I managed four hours of fitful sleep punctuated by disturbing dreams of Avril Wilts' corpse chasing me down the boardwalk. The dreams got me up and dressed before the first rays of daylight. Dawn broke hot and humid as I walked on the boardwalk from the hotel to the pier. And yes, I'm embarrassed to admit I periodically looked behind me in case Avril's corpse was behind me.

I sat on the same wooden bench at the end of the pier as usual and watched the fishermen casting and recasting their lines into the placid, minty green Atlantic. Was I gratified or horrified that I'd been right all along that Avril framed Mariel and murdered Simon? Maybe a bit of both. The gory scene and the words typed on the bloody suicide note rolled continuously through my mind like a horror show filmstrip. I couldn't put my finger on it, but something was off about Avril's death. Hopefully, some strong coffee and the Yentas' take on things would put things into their proper perspective.

Two hours later, I laid the latest edition of the *East Coast Apparel News* across the Yenta table. The headline above the fold read: *Swim Show Slaying Suspect Succumbs in Suicide.*

Joan raised her coffee cup and toasted me. "Once again, our Triple M had it right all along."

I blew the air out of my cheeks. "I want to be right regarding Avril's guilt, but something's not Kosher about her death."

Sonia stroked her chin. "What's bothering you?"

I held out my hands. "You all witnessed Avril Wilts in action. Pushy, relentless, demanding, in your face, daring you to defy or deny her. That is not a personality type likely to commit suicide."

Queenie dipped her head. "I agree, Hol. She didn't seem the type, but you have to admit that from what we witnessed, it was pretty damned convincing that she chose that route."

Hope grimaced. "Let's say, for the sake of argument, she killed herself. How does a person decide that taking their own life is their only viable option?"

Sonia stroked her chin. "If it's the only way for them to face the consequences of their actions."

Joan sneered. "You ask me, she took the coward's way out."

Queenie tapped her index finger on the tip of her nose. "Nosiree. You're wrong, Joanie. I don't have the guts it takes to stick the barrel of a gun to my neck and pull the trigger."

Sonia formed her fingers into the shape of a pistol. "You'd better be damned sure you want to do it, because once you pull the trigger, it's a done deal; no changing your mind or chickening out."

I nodded. "Yeah. My point exactly. It might be the timing that's off kilter."

Sonia asked, "Do you mean the estimated time of death the coroner made?"

I funneled my lips. "Yep. According to Walter Seiden, Avril was in her booth the morning of her death and left in a rush. But if we go by Jazzy's timeline based on her evaluation of the physical condition of the corpse, Avril was already dead."

Joan widened her eyes. "And the alternative theory to the way she died is...?"

I tapped a teaspoon on the edge of the table. "I aim to figure it out."

Considering that it was the last full day of the market, we were steadily busy all morning. But after lunch, the trade show buyer traffic ground to a crawl. Since we had ample help in the booth, I went back to my hotel room to scratch the Avril suicide itch before it drove me mad. I took a legal pad out of my messenger bag and made a rough sketch of yesterday's scene to jog the issue niggling in the back of my mind to come forward. I stared at the sketch until my eyes almost crossed. I held the pen in my left hand and tapped the sketch, certain the answer was somewhere. And suddenly it dawned on me. Avril was holding the gun in *her right hand instead of her left!*

I grabbed the cell phone and dialed Jazzy Jones.

"Miami-Dade Medical Examiner's office. This is Assistant Medical Examiner Dr. Jasmine Jones."

"Jazzy, it's Holly Schlivnik."

Jazzy laughed. "Hey, girl. You didn't get enough of me last night?"

"Good guess."

"So, what's goin' on?"

"I've been going over the deets of Avril Wilts' death in my mind, and something's not Kosher."

"Such as?"

"For starters, Mo and I tried to see Avril around lunchtime on the day she died, but she wasn't in her booth. Walter Seiden's booth is next to hers, and we asked him if he'd seen her. He said she came in sometime in the morning, but she left in a hurry. We asked if he knew what time she left. He said he was working with a customer when Avril left, and he wasn't sure of what time. He promised to tell her to see me when she got back. Either she never returned to her booth, or if she did, I have no way of knowing whether or not he gave her the message. Either way, she never contacted me. The next time I came in contact with her was when I discovered her body in the blue car. But if we go by your timeline based on your evaluation of the physical condition of the corpse, Avril was already dead by the time Walter said he saw her in her booth. Something else was bugging me, but it wasn't clear as to what. So, I sketched the scene, hoping to jog my memory, and it worked. Jazzy, Avril Wilts was holding the gun in her *right hand*, but she was left-handed."

Scientist Jazzy logically reasoned, "She might have been ambidextrous."

"It's possible, but I doubt it. Avril and I spent some time together in LA. We worked on several of the same industry committees and ate lunch together a few times. She did *everything* using her left hand. She ate, signed the credit card slip, and opened her car door, all using her left hand. I'm a leftie too, and we swapped southpaw stories of how difficult it is to be a leftie in a right-handed world. I'm telling you, Avril Wilts didn't have the necessary strength and dexterity to shoot herself holding a gun in her right hand any more than I."

"Then somebody worked pretty damned hard to make it look like a suicide. Any particular candidate come to mind?"

I held up my right wrist and glanced at my watch. Suddenly, a vision of someone doing the same thing at the fashion show cocktail party flashed like a klieg light in my brain. In a moment of clarity, the gears in my brain meshed, and everything fell into place. How could I have been so blind and gotten it so wrong?

"Jazzy, I had it all wrong. It's *Walter Seiden*. I can't believe it took me this long, but I finally remembered that, *like me and every other leftie, he wears his watch on his right wrist.*" I sighed. "Avril's death is on me." The guilty weight of responsibility was a gut punch that twisted my innards into knots. "If his being left-handed had dawned on me sooner, Avril might not be dead. Did you receive the fingerprint report yet?"

"Yeah. Hang on a sec, and let me grab it. Okay, am I looking for something in particular?"

"How many sets of fingerprints are on the gun, the suicide note, and the newspaper?"

"Lemme see. Two sets. Avril's and a second set. No match to any in the state system. So, whoever it is doesn't have a police record."

"Were the second sets the same prints for all three items or different per item?"

"Not the same."

I slammed the heel of my hand on the desk. "Dammit, that muddies the water." I snapped my fingers. "Contact the Department of Defense and see if Walter Seiden, Avril Wilts, and the twins were ever in the military. If one of them was, request their fingerprints and compare them to the unidentified ones on those three items."

"Lemme make a few calls, and I'll get back to you."

Jazzy called back an hour later. It just seemed like a week.

"Walter Seiden was an Army Ranger. We've requested his prints be sent to our lab and a copy of them to Sergeant Yieh."

"Will the labs get them today?"

"The Miami-Dade Chief Medical Examiner *personally* made the request, so yes. I'll call you and Mo Lehrman if there's a match."

I paced in my hotel room like an expectant father for the next hour. Before I wore a groove in the carpet, I went back to our booth to keep busy and not drive myself crazy with anticipation.

Two hours later, while I was working, Jazzy left me a voicemail. I finished showing the lines and listened to the message. "Seiden's fingerprints weren't a match to those on the coconut, the newspaper, or the suicide note."

Dammit! I snapped a pencil in half. *Was it possible that Avril killed herself? Could I be so wrong? Wait a Cincinnati minute. Jazzy forgot the gun.*

As though she read my mind, Jazzy said, "But Seiden was either in a hurry or got sloppy. His left thumbprint and index fingerprint are a perfect match to the second set of prints on the gun. We nailed him, Holly, thanks to you. I already sent a voicemail to Detective Lehrman."

I glanced across the aisle to Luce's booth, and my stomach lurched. She could be Walter's next victim. I texted her to trust me and to stay away from Walter, and not to go anywhere alone with him.

As I was about to text Mo, my phone pinged a text from him. He asked me to meet him at the rooftop garden at my hotel in half an hour, and said it was important. I grabbed my messenger bag, said goodbye to the Yentas, and headed for the hotel.

Chapter Forty-One

Twenty minutes later, I took the hotel elevator to the rooftop. An arrow above a sketch of flora and fauna pointed toward the rooftop garden. I followed the signs down a narrow corridor. I opened the door marked with the same sketch, and my jaw dropped.

A serpentine path meandered through a riotous rainbow of colorful blooms, tropical plants, and trees. Recessed waterfalls were strategically placed between the sections of the rectangular, lush garden. Piped-in tapes of tropical bird calls brought guests to a rainforest nestled into the heart of South Beach. Chaise lounges, chairs, and tables were arranged in each section for visitors to relax or chat while taking in the garden sights.

Mo was seated next to a huge wedge of agave bordered by Cuban oregano plants on his left side, a banana tree on his right, and adjacent to a coconut palm tree in the left quadrant, facing the rail overlooking the Atlantic. I leaned down, and Mo's five o'clock shadow scratched my lips as I brushed them across his roughened cheek. I held up my watch. "I was finishing an appointment when you texted. You said it was important, so I rushed over. I guess Jazzy called you. She called me, too."

Mo looked at me strangely, as though I was speaking in tongues. "I didn't text you. You texted me to meet you on the hotel rooftop. And you said it was important, so I dropped everything and raced across town."

I arched a brow. "If you didn't text me, and I didn't text you, who sent the texts? The text fairy?"

Before Mo could reply, Walter Seiden, clutching an M9 pistol in his left hand and sporting a maniacal grin on his kisser, suddenly popped up a few feet from us like a jack-in-the-box on LSD. I almost wet myself when he jumped out from behind a huge bougainvillea cattycorner to the rail overlooking the ocean. "Surprise, lovebirds! It's me, *your favorite neighborhood text fairy*. Now that the two guests of honor are present, their farewell party can begin."

I waved my hands around the garden. "How did you do it?"

Walter shrugged. "I've been controlling your phone."

"How?"

"My PhD. in electrical engineering came in quite handy."

Walter grinned evilly and pointed to Mo. "The day at the food court, *after I saved you from him*, you and I had coffee. Your cell phone was next to mine on the table, and I cloned yours. I tracked you the way a lion tracks its prey. Fortunately, you made it easy. You're a creature of habit who does the same daily pre-dawn walk."

He tapped his right index finger into the small of his chest. "I was the one on the bicycle."

Walter glanced at Mo. "Not to be critical of your choices in women, but your girlfriend is an odd one. She named her dog *Sigmund Freud*? Who names a *dog* after a shrink? She not only called the person watching him while she was away, but they also put the dog on the phone, and she and the dog carried on a conversation. I must have laughed for an hour."

Walter pointed to me. "And another thing, pal, you might not know it, but you're not the only rooster in her hen house. She sweet-talks to some guy on the West Coast named Buddy." Walter winked at Mo. "Show some gratitude, man. Thanks to me, in a few minutes, she will be yours alone for all eternity."

Mo surreptitiously reached for his holstered semi-automatic pistol.

Regrettably, not surreptitiously enough...

Walter made a gimme motion using his right hand. "Detective, using only your index finger, take your pistol out of the holster nice and slow and easy. Lay it on the ground and kick it to me."

Mo lasered Walter with a, pardon the pun, murderous glare. He kept his hand on the gun's grip and ignored Walter's order.

Walter aimed his gun barrel at my forehead. "You've got to the count of three, Detective, to do the smart thing or I'll blow your girlfriend's head off and won't lose a minute of sleep."

I performed my best ventriloquist imitation, whispering through gritted teeth. "He's going to kill us anyway, so don't give him the satisfaction of an execution. You might as well shoot the bastard and go out taking him with us."

Mo whispered back, "No. I'll do as he says. You keep him talking and distract him to buy us some time while I figure out a way to overpower him."

Walter widened his stance into a shooting position. "One, two..."

Mo yelled, "Okay! Don't shoot." He unholstered his weapon as instructed and kicked it to Walter.

Walter pushed Mo's gun behind him with his heel. "Wise choice, Detective. Now, stand up and step into the aisle. Slowly remove the pistol from your ankle holster and kick it to me."

This time around, Mo immediately complied.

I whispered, "By any chance, is a third gun strapped to your other leg?"

Mo laughed a mirthless, gallows-humor chuckle. "No such luck. Now, it's your turn at bat. Keep him talking."

As it turned out, instead of shooting us dead the moment Mo kicked both guns to him, Walter became a chatterbox.

He grinned. "Holly, thank you for not guessing it was me for so long, and for providing ways to frame others to look guilty." He laughed. "You were so helpful, I began to consider you my accomplice."

Fanfreakingtastic. Not only was this bastard going to kill me, but the jerk insulted my intelligence first.

He sighed. "It's too bad you didn't agree to go out with me. Then only you would have died." He aimed his gun at Mo. "Avril and your lover boy would have been spared." Walter's face contorted into an ugly sneer. "So, Miss High and Mighty big shot manufacturer, a lowly sales rep like me wasn't good enough for you?"

I lunged, but Mo clamped a hand on the scruff of my neck and whispered in my ear, "Down, girl. It serves no purpose to react and give him the satisfaction of seeing he got your goat."

Walter looked at Mo. "But since I didn't get my chance with your girlfriend before, I've got a second one now. And this time it will be even better, because now *you'll be my audience*." He licked his chops. "So, this is the way our little performance is gonna play out. You're both going to die in a murder/suicide lovers' spat, but not before you, Detective, watch me ravage your lover." He giggled. "After all, only a poor host doesn't provide entertainment at your farewell party."

I swallowed the bile that came up from my stomach and forced a sincere look of concern onto my face. "Walter, you're an intelligent man. Consider the step you're taking carefully before you do something you can't undo. The police will figure it out. If you're a cop killer, it's a four-alarm fire and all hands-on deck. The police will be relentless and never give up until they find you. When they do, and trust me, they will, even God won't be able to help you. If you don't care about yourself, consider your kids. They've already lost their mother. And next to lose you? Do you want to do this to your children? Leave us and make a run for it. Take your children and disappear. There are plenty of countries with no reciprocal extradition agreements with the United States."

Walter burst out laughing. "You win the Miss Gullible prize. I've never been married, and if I sired any children, I'm not aware of them. I made up the sappy, stupid story so you'd go on a pity date with me. It was all a ruse to get you alone to eliminate you and out of my hair for good."

I gasped. "*Nothing you told me was true*?"

Walter nodded. "Almost all of it was a tall tale. The only truthful things are that I earned a PhD. in electrical engineering, I am a bike rider, Simon did steal my line, and I was out of work for a year and lost everything. I've been plotting to kill Simon for over a year. Either the timing was off, or there was no one to frame. But thanks to your, Mariel Levine's, and Avril's help, this time, it all fell into place."

I said, "After your big shoving match, it was a wonder you convinced Simon to go any place with you, let alone to the storage room." I bit my lip. "Unless you drugged him, you needed help." And then the gears meshed. The wheels inside my head started spinning, and the rest of the puzzle pieces finally fit. I squawked as loud as a wet hen. "Son of a bitch! You and Avril *conspired* to kill Simon."

Walter grinned. "Bravo! I'm impressed you figured it out. It was serendipity that Avril's booth was next to mine. Once she shared their history, and I realized her level of hatred for Simon matched mine, I owned her. She not only agreed to help murder Simon but *thanked me for the opportunity*. She lured Simon to the storage room with the promise of sex. She played her part, and then I killed the bastard using the coconut I took out of the trash to frame Mariel for the crime."

Walter looked me in the eye and, I'd swear, I detected a thread of remorse in his tone of voice. "I tried to warn you multiple times to back off, but you didn't take the hint, and now you and lover boy are going to die, and it's all your fault."

I asked, "How did you get Avril into her car?"

Walter grinned. "I told her that when I tried to start my car that morning to go to the convention center, the battery was dead. The Auto Rescuers quoted a two-hour wait for a tow truck, so I called a cab and left the car at home. I told Avril I had jumper cables in the trunk of my car. I asked her to do me a favor and drive me home so I could use her battery to jumpstart my car, and she agreed. I waited until she was behind the wheel and had her seatbelt on." Walter pointed to a spot on his neck. "Then I reached over and jabbed my index finger as hard as I could into the carotid on the side of her neck. She went out like a light. Once she was unconscious, I got out of the car and walked around to the driver's side and opened the door. I pulled my sports jacket over my knuckles to absorb the gunshot residue. I put the gun in her right hand, covered it with mine, and aimed for the small of her neck. I leaned to the side to avoid the blood splatter. Then I put my index finger over hers, and she pulled the trigger. I locked the car and left her there."

Walter reached behind him and grabbed a coiled rope. He motioned for Mo to turn around and put his hands behind him. Walter tossed me the rope and pointed to the coconut palm. "You're a sailor, so tie lover boy's wrists into a tight constrictor knot and lash him to the trunk of the palm tree, facing the entrance to the garden so he'll enjoy a front row seat to watch everything I'm going to do to you."

Mo refused to turn around, and Walter smashed the butt of his gun into Mo's jaw. Mo reared back and spat a mouthful of blood into Walter's eyes, and Walter screeched like a little girl. The damned fool scrubbed his eyes, using the heel of his free hand, and rubbed the blood into his eyes even more. Walter staggered as sloppily as a drunk, but he remarkably managed to hold onto the gun.

Mo gave me the opening I prayed for. I two-handed the rope and threw it overhand. The knot that kept the rope coiled hit Walter with a satisfying loud thwack on the bridge of his nose. Blood gushed out of his broken nose like a geyser. Walter waved the gun, but he couldn't see where to aim it. Enraged, he played the odds and started shooting indiscriminately, in the hopes he'd hit one of us with blind luck. At six feet tall, Mo was an easier target. I yelled, "*Moisés, abájalo, ahora!*" Mo dropped to the floor and rolled behind the bougainvillea.

For once, being a shortie worked to my advantage. I hit the deck and rolled onto my back. I turned my ankles out straight so the balls of my feet sat perpendicular to Walter's kneecaps. I pulled my knees up to my chest, powered using my calves, pushed out, and kicked Walter in the knees as hard as I could. His knees buckled. He pinwheeled his arms, trying to keep his balance, and he dropped the gun.

While Walter was distracted using his feet to feel around the floor for the gun, I rolled onto my side and grabbed a coconut from under the palm tree. I sat up, used both hands to raise the coconut high enough for a maximum arc, and heaved it at Walter's head. The coconut hit him hard and right between the eyes.

Walter's head whipped back, and his body teetered. He backpedaled into the railing, and the momentum carried him over. As he plummeted to the ground, I waved goodbye and said, "*Adios, amigo.*"

The echo of Walter's terrified screams ceased when his body slammed onto the asphalt road below. Mo and I peered over the railing and watched Walter's body bounce like a beachball across the road and break apart.

Mo danced a little jig and asked, "Where'd you learn all the fancy footwork?"

"Martial arts and MacGyver."

Mo narrowed his eyes. "Come again?"

"Dad made sure his children could defend themselves by enrolling us in Krav Maga starting as kindergarteners. And growing up, we kids watched all the classic TV shows with our parents, including MacGyver, who taught me to think on my feet and be creative by using anything available as a weapon."

Mo put his arms out and hands up in front of his body as though protecting himself from a blow.

He grinned. "Man, remind me to never piss you off."

Chapter Forty-Two

That Mo and I lived to tell the tale was cause for celebration, but the gruesome deaths of three swimwear industry colleagues hit a little too close to home and got me where I live. While the three victims were certainly no angels, their violent deaths still diminished the entire industry. So, cracking open a bottle of bubbly and toasting one another's good fortune was as disrespectful as dancing on one of their graves.

By the time the CSI and coroner's teams cleared the scene and Mo and I gave our statements to the MBPD homicide detective assigned to the case, it was way after dark when we were allowed to leave the hotel rooftop.

We followed the EMT orders and waited over an hour for our turn in the emergency room at Miami Beach General Hospital to get Mo's split lip stitched. By then, we were both too exhausted to see well-meaning family and friends, but too emotionally wrought to be alone.

Considering the horrible experience we'd been through, food should have been the last thing on our minds. Remarkably, we were both famished, but with Mo's fat lip, our eating choices were limited.

Mo was cagey as he put the top down and aimed the trusty muscle car heading south on A1A. The humidity was high enough to give the heavy air a chewy texture. A light rain had bathed the southern section of the city and washed away the grit in the air an hour earlier, so the evening temperature cooled down to a balmy eighty degrees. I tilted my head back and marveled at the twinkling scatter of stars and the full strawberry moon dominating the inky black sky.

It was nine-thirty when Mo used a key card to open the gate to the boaters-only parking structure at the Bayside Boatyard and Marina. He pulled into an open space and put the top up. We walked toward the end of the wooden pier and stood in front of iconic Mama Miceli's Pizzeria. Mama Miceli's was a favorite hangout of ours, once upon a time. We often ate at Miceli's after a day of sailing.

Mo grinned. "Do you remember the first time we entered the holiday boat parade?"

I slapped my cheeks. "Are you kidding? How could I ever forget? We decorated your sailboat with blue and white Hanukkah lights and hoisted a Jewish star made of blue and white lights to the top of the mast."

"And when it was our turn to sail into the bay, the marina dockmaster said we couldn't participate because our boat didn't meet the event decorations requirements."

I laughed, "He changed his tune when you called your cousin Benjamin, the lawyer, and put him on the phone with the dockmaster."

"Yep, Bennie threatened him with a discrimination lawsuit that the dockmaster had no chance of winning. That lawsuit would have bankrupted the marina."

"We never had that problem again."

Mo motioned to the Miceli's entrance and sighed. "It's weird being with you and not eating at Mama M's." He pointed to his fat lip. "But even if I could get the slice into my mouth without busting the stitches, the spices would burn my lip."

I nodded. "You're right. It's not worth it to risk breaking your stitches over a pizza." I looked around the dark pier. "So, if we're not eating at Miceli's, why are we here?"

He arched a brow and crooked his index finger. "Follow me."

We walked to the apex of the pier and turned right. The bright red, white, and blue flashing lights of Uncle Izzy's Ice Cream Emporium lit up the sky as brightly as the fireworks displays on the Fourth of July.

I squealed with delight. "An Uncle Izzy trough! The ultimate comfort food."

We entered and sat in a red vinyl tufted booth for two, separated by a Formica table covered with a white oilcloth tablecloth featuring free-floating ice cream cones and sundaes. Hundreds of plastic ice cream cones in a rainbow of colors dangled from the ceiling and were framed by red, pink, and white ice cream cone wallpaper.

We ordered the house specialty, a tin trough filled to the brim with scoops of rocky road, Jamoca almond fudge, interspersed with sliced bananas, vanilla, and peanut butter brickle ice cream. The gluttonous gourmet treat was covered with real whipped cream, drizzled with hot fudge, and topped by two maraschino cherries.

I giggled. "Imagine our mothers' faces."

Mo rolled his eyes. "And the lecture we would endure about eating junk food instead of a nutritious meal."

Ten minutes later, bells, whistles, and sirens sounded to signal the arrival of the ice cream extravaganza. The lavish feast was carried to our table by four servers. Each one hoisted a corner of the trough over their head and oinked like pigs as they placed the frozen treat in the middle of the table. Two waiters tied paper bibs around our necks, and the other two handed us tablespoon-sized ladles. All conversation stopped as we eagerly dug in, like two people who hadn't eaten in a week, and finished every bit, including the cherries.

Stuffed to the gills, we strolled along the pier to burn off the meal, stopping to window shop as something caught our eye. We reached the end of the pier, and I asked, "Not that I minded, but I'm curious. Another Uncle Izzy's is only a few blocks from the hotel. Why come all the way out here?"

We turned north onto a path that led to a gated marina, and he pulled me closer. "Because we can't take an evening sail from that location, but since this one is on the pier next to the marina where our Universal is docked, we can."

My concerned eyes searched his. "It's been one helluva day. Are you up for a sail?"

He shrugged. "I'd have to be in a coma not to be up for a sail."

I licked my index finger and held it up in the air. "The prevailing wind is pretty weak and coming in from the northwest. It's only blowing around five knots at most, so you'll be lucky to catch enough to sail into the bay, and only if we get a strong crosswind. If not, either go out under power or risk sitting in irons at the mouth of the bay until high tide."

He patted my arm. "You're still my best navigator. We'll motor out into the bay. If there's no crosswind, we'll just take a spin around the perimeter and motor back to the dock." He wiggled his eyebrows. "Or, we don't have to leave the slip at all."

I cuffed his shoulder. "The hell we won't! I want to see this baby in action."

He took a set of keys from his pants pocket and opened a security gate marked number twenty, the last basin before entering the main channel. He led me down a well-lit gangplank to the last slip on the south side of the basin, where a gleaming white sailboat trimmed in teak took my breath away.

I pointed to the stern and read the boat name out loud. "*Esperanza Nueva*. New Hope." I turned to Mo. "What a wonderful name. Did the boat come with that name?"

Mo shook his head. "No. The previous owner never named her." He smiled. "I'm so glad you like the name we chose. Given our family history, it tells our story in just two words."

Mo scrambled up a three-rung ladder and climbed over the portside midship between the stern and the cabin. He offered his hand and guided me across the threshold. He gave the fifty-cent tour, and I didn't know where to look first.

The main salon served as the heart and focal point of the layout. The well-equipped galley and breakfast nook, which comfortably seated six, were situated adjacent to the main salon. An office next to the guest's berth was located down the hall, near storage closets. The master suite featured a walk-in closet, a separate head and full bath with a shower, and was flanked by two sizable V-berths. Stairs leading to the engine room below were positioned midway down the hall. This was no ordinary sailboat; it was a floating mansion.

I curved my lips into an appreciative smile. "This is some boat. The slip fees and upkeep alone must be a fortune. MBPD detectives are apparently much better paid than those with the LAPD."

Mo waved the concept off. "Nobody gets rich on a cop's salary. Dad and I split all the fees." He swept an arm around the main salon. "Once Dad opened his first store, my parents lived as frugally as possible and put every penny of profit back into the business. My sisters wore hand-me-down clothes, and we ate a lot of rice and beans for the first five years. After the tenth store opened, one of Dad's sportswear representatives suggested that he enroll in an adult education investment class that his wife taught. Dad enrolled, and it changed his life. He not only learned the best way to invest business profits for maximum return, but he also learned how much to take out of the business, how to invest his money, and how to diversify his personal portfolio. And he shared everything he learned with his best friend...*your father*. They bought commercial buildings together and invested in the same stocks. And they allowed me to invest along with them on a smaller scale."

Mo rapped his knuckles on a teak table in the main salon. "We've done pretty well, knock wood."

"How well are we talking about?"

"The daddios are loaded, and if I wanted to retire, after a few lifestyle changes, it's doable."

Holy guacamole.

"Do our mothers know?"

Mo shook his head. "Only that they're extremely comfortable, but not that they're filthy rich."

I laughed. "Oh, to be a fly on the wall the day my mother finds out. It's a toss-up whether she'll hug Dad or hit him over the head with a cast-iron frying pan."

Mo fingered his rumpled suit jacket. "Let's get changed and go for the sail before it gets too late."

I patted myself down. "I don't have a change of clothes with me, and yours are way too big."

Mo ushered me into the master suite and opened the walk-in closet door.

He handed me my old boat bag, which contained my sailing gear. "You kept my boat bag all these years?" I held it by my fingertips as if it had cooties and handed it back to him. "I'm sure you haven't been celibate all this time, and I'd rather not wear anything you let one of your lady friends use to go sailing in."

Mo recoiled in horror. "How could you even suggest I'd do something as tacky as that?"

I gave him the stink eye. "Why else would you keep it?"

A longing for what might have been softened his tone. "To keep a part of you and everything we once shared." He made a ta-da with his hands. "As long as I kept your boat bag, I could still hope that a future for us together was possible. *Is it*?"

His eyes bored into mine.

The intensity of his stare was so strong, I had to look away.

He turned my head to face him with his index finger.

He wanted an answer.

I could barely breathe, let alone reply.

I'd lose my mind being so close to him any longer.

I checked the time.

Eleven-thirty.

I plotted my escape.

And miraculously managed to keep the quiver out of my voice.

"Mo, I'm exhausted. I bet you are, too. I'm staying in town for a few extra days. Let's plan an all-day sail next week."

He nodded. "Okay. That makes a lot of sense. A well-planned day sail to one of the nearby keys is a much better option."

Thank the Goddess for small favors.

I shouldered my messenger bag. "Then let's get going. The sooner you get me back to the hotel, the sooner you'll get home, and we'll both get more sleep. After a day like today, we can both use it."

He grinned. "Getting more sleep is an excellent idea." He swept an arm around the spacious room. "The good news is that I am already home. I sold my condo a few months ago and live full-time on the boat. So, to maximize our number of zzzs, I suggest that we spend the night here."

Crap on a crumpet.

As Hamlet so eloquently put it, I was hoisted by my own petard.

I opened my mouth to object, but he put a shushing finger to my lips and pulled me into his arms. "Stay with me tonight." He whispered, "You're the only one I ever want to share a sunrise with."

Chapter Forty-Three

Mo dropped me off at the hotel the next morning on his way to a mandatory post-incident psychological evaluation at MBPD Headquarters. I had just enough time to take a quick shower, change clothes, and stop at the hotel lobby newsstand before meeting the Yentas for coffee. What can I say? When it comes to that man, my heart overrules my head, and all rational plans get thrown out the window.

I slid into my seat and mouthed *thanks* to Hope for handing me the cup of steaming hot coffee. I took two sips and spread the front page of the latest edition of the *East Coast Apparel News* across the center of the table.

The headline above the fold read:

Mermaid Maven Crushes Coconut Killer

The normal menagerie of motormouth magpies sat stunned in gape-mouthed silence as I detailed the events of the day before.

I finished telling the sordid story and mentally prepared for the Yentas' saucy commentaries.

As usual, they came through.

The Yentas stood, chorused, "*Bravo, Bravo*!" and raised their cups in a salute.

I bowed from the waist.

Sonia flashed the V for victory sign. "Congratulations, Madame Triple M. Your successful case-closing record is still intact. And now you're the undisputed super sleuth of the swimwear industry from *coast to coast*."

I bunched my shoulders. "Technically, I was only half right. I didn't make the connection that Avril and Walter conspired to kill Simon and frame Mariel right away. I always believed *Avril* was Simon's killer. But it wasn't until her so-called suicide made no sense that I realized Walter was up to his neck in Avril's death. While Walter was the mastermind, with the animus between him and Simon, he couldn't get Simon alone to get the deed done by himself. Avril had issues with both Mariel and Simon, so she was the perfect partner to commit the crime and the frame."

Sonia rubbed her chin. "And Walter was always two steps ahead of you?"

I pursed my lips. "I'm embarrassed to admit it, but...yes."

"How?"

"With his PhD. in Electrical Engineering, he knew how to clone my phone. He was aware of everything I planned in real time. He tracked me and countered every move I made. He fed me false information to get the reactions he wanted."

Hope shivered. "How creepy."

I nodded. "And tragic. Once Mariel was cleared of the charges, Walter needed a new patsy to frame. The only two remaining were Avril and Lucinda. Walter no doubt listened in on my conversation with Jazzy Jones the day I suggested she inquire if any of the suspects had been in the military. Once Jazzy confirmed Walter was an Army Ranger, the jig was up. He realized I tagged him as the killer, and I inadvertently signed Avril's death warrant."

Hope asked, "How does that make you to blame for her death?"

"Because Walter knew Avril was my number one suspect, so I made it easy for him to set her up." I hung my head. "I might as well have pulled the trigger."

Hope asked, "How did he get Avril to go with him? Did Walter follow Avril to her car and overpower her?"

Sonia shook her head. "If he did, he'd be taking a huge risk that she would scream her head off, and somebody might come to her rescue and take him down."

I nodded. "You're right. He didn't overpower her at all. He got her to go willingly."

Queenie asked, "How?"

I said, "He told her when he got into his car that morning to go to the convention center that his battery was dead. He said that the Auto Rescuers quoted a two-hour wait for a tow truck, so he called a cab and left his car at home. He told Avril he had jumper cables in his car trunk and asked her to do him a favor and drive him home so he could use her battery to jumpstart his. She agreed. He waited until she was behind the wheel and had her seatbelt on. Then he reached across and jabbed his index finger as hard as he could into the side of her neck in the carotid. She went out like a light. Once she was unconscious, he got out of the car, walked around to the driver's side, and opened the door. He pulled his sports jacket over his knuckles to absorb the gunshot residue. He put the gun in her right hand, covered her hand with his, and aimed the gun barrel at the small of her neck. He leaned to the side to avoid the blood splatter. Then he put his index finger over hers, and she pulled the trigger. He locked the car doors and went back to his booth and lied to Mo and me about when he saw her last."

Queenie said, "Talk about cold-blooded and heartless."

Joanie whistled. "Yeah, but he was certainly thorough. The guy thought of everything."

I shook my head. "Almost, but not everything. Walter would have gotten away with both murders, but he planted the gun in Avril's wrong hand and didn't wear gloves, so there were two of his fingerprints on the gun. And most of all, he didn't understand that a personality like hers would have had no remorse, so the suicide note didn't ring true to her. And it's a good thing he made those mistakes. When the police searched his car, in addition to receipts for a gold wedding band and the .38 Special Lady Smith pistol, they also found a suitcase stuffed with ten thousand dollars in cash under his clothes, his passport, and a first-class one-way airline ticket to Brazil, all hidden in the wheel well in the trunk."

Joan smirked. "So, how'd you manage to save the day?"

"A triple threat of Martial Arts, Moxy, and MacGyver."

Queenie tapped the tip of her nose. "Bullpucky. Cut out the crap, sister. The truth? You're just one of those people who thrive on defying the odds and living on the edge of disaster."

I sniffed my righteous indignation. "Potato, Potahto. Tomato, Tomahto."

Hope scratched the crown of her head. "So, since you saved Detective Lehrman's tush, where does it leave you with the rest of him?"

I shrugged.

If I only had a clue...

Sonia rubbed her chin. "An old proverb says once you save somebody's life, they are indebted to you for the rest of their days, but through the act of saving their life, you are now responsible for their life."

Queenie smirked. "That explains the shortage of Good Samaritans among mankind."

I rolled my eyes.

Joan slapped the table and laughed. "It's a good thing, Hol, that you didn't hear the proverb before your heroics, or you might not have saved his bacon."

Everyone is a wannabe comedian.

I checked the time. "Ladies, on that note, before we go to the convention center, I want to thank each of you for your hard work at the market. Mermaid is off to a great start for another successful season, thanks to all of you. Once I take care of a few things at the booth, I'm leaving early today. I am staying in Miami for an extra week to spend time with my family. It's been a long time since we've seen one another, so if any issues come up requiring immediate attention, reach out to either Queenie or Gary."

As the group rose to leave, I tugged on Queenie's shirtsleeve. "Before we get to the booth, let's decide the best way to let Lauren go. Instead of taking a confrontational approach and burning a bridge unnecessarily, let's just say we don't need a full-time showroom manager and we realize that she needs a full-time job."

I grinned. "We take a page out of Nana's game book and say one door closes, but another one opens. From the tragic three deaths, an opportunity for the twins appeared. We suggest it is the perfect time for them to move up the ladder and open their own sales organization. Since Luce is experienced with all of Simon's and Walter's lines, those manufacturers will jump at the chance to hire her. The Tigress management is in a terrible position to lose someone as key as Avril, and will also be open to hiring the girls. We give Lauren three months' severance and part as friends." I laughed. "By the time we're through, she'll thank us for letting her go. How does that game plan sound?"

"It's a shrewd way to make us heroes instead of hard asses." Smart-alec Queenie snarked, "The only fly in the ointment is if the twins realize that each person representing those lines before them all ended up dead."

Chapter Forty-Four

One Week Later

The cruise ship pulled into port and dropped anchor. Loudspeakers on the main deck crackled to life, and a deep male voice made an announcement. "Until we meet again, the captain and crew of the *Fiesta de Florida* thank you for cruising with us and wish you a fond farewell."

We joined the throng of disembarking passengers. Mo and I said our goodbyes to our families, retrieved our luggage, and headed for the guest parking structure. We found Mo's convertible and stowed our luggage in the trunk. Mo put the top down and drove west on I-195.

I whistled my admiration. "That was some retirement party the daddios put on. Leave it to them to win the Monte Carlo Senior Division tournament and spend their winnings on a three-day cruise from Miami to the Bahamas for both our families."

Mo said, "Considering the time difference, it's astonishing how quickly they were able to plan the entire celebration on the phone for so many people."

I counted on my fingers. "Seven Lehrman family members and five from the Schlivnik clan. Dad called my brother Jerry, who works as a dealer on a sister ship for the same cruise line. Dad gave Jerry the details around dawn, Miami time, and when Dad woke up the next morning, Jerry had everything arranged."

Mo laughed. "The daddios were the rock stars of the cruise. They had the crowd and the crew dancing in a conga line every night."

I said, "And when the bandleader found out your dad is a Cuban jazz aficionado, they performed a tribute to Cuban jazz musicians in his honor."

Mo said, "That was amazing, but when the bandleader invited Dad to sit in on a set and play his version of Arturo Sandoval's biggest hits on the trumpet, it was one of the biggest honors of Dad's life. Arturo Sandoval is Dad's idol."

Mo grinned. "Something tells me that your dad had a hand in arranging that."

"There is no question about it. Mike Schlivnik made it happen. I've never been on a cruise before. How about you?"

Mo shook his head. "Nope. This was my first one, too. Our parents went on several, so to me, a cruise was strictly an older person's kind of vacation."

"I had the same impression. But it turns out we were wrong. There was something for every age group."

We transitioned onto Westbound State Highway 112. A sign advised that the Miami International Airport was 9.9 miles ahead. Mo sighed and curled his fingers around mine. "It's hard to believe how fast the time flew by."

"Time flies when you're having fun."

"And now you're leaving."

I said, "All good things must come to an end."

Mo glanced at me. "Why?"

I shrugged. "Because that's the way life is. Nothing bad lasts forever, but nothing good lasts forever, either."

Mo said, "The good things won't come to an end if we don't let them slip away. That's the trouble with people. They get a chance to be happy and pay no attention. And in the blink of an eye, the chance slips through their fingers. They can't figure out how it happened and spend the rest of their lives regretting every coulda, woulda, and shoulda. Your Nana used to say...?"

I smiled at the memory. "Regret is the worst human emotion because it is the one we can usually do nothing about."

Mo nodded. "Yeah, that's it. She was a wise woman. We should pay attention to what she said."

"Meaning?"

"Meaning, since we got a second chance at happiness, it's criminal to blow it."

I rolled my eyes. "Come on, Mo. Get real. Ours is an impossible situation, and in your heart of hearts, you know it. I can't, no; I won't give up my life in LA and move back to Miami. I've worked too hard to walk away from everything I've built."

"I'd never ask you to do such a thing. Your business is in LA, and you need to be there to run it. I get it. But I can be a cop anyplace."

I clucked my tongue. "But your *life* and your *family* are *in Miami*. Don't you see that *one of us has to give up the life they've built for us to be together?* And eventually, the love turns into resentment, and a beautiful relationship gets destroyed."

Mo smacked the steering wheel with the heel of his hand. "*No! You're wrong.*" He softened the tone of his voice. "I *live* in Miami now, but *home* for me would be wherever you are."

I shook my head. "It's more complicated."

"No, it isn't. Marry me. It's that simple. I'm taking some time off and coming to Los Angeles."

"Why?"

"To work this all out."

I held out my hands as though fending off a blow. "Whoa. That's not a great idea. We need time and distance apart to evaluate if this is love or just lust."

Mo laughed. "Dios Mio, if it isn't both, we're in trouble. Okay, instead of right now, I'll make the reservations for the end of August. That gives you time to finalize your sample lines, then go to the New York, Dallas, and Hawaii markets. Present the lines and get your initial order commitments. And time to think about us. How does that plan sound?"

My back stiffened as we approached the East Okeechobee Road exit.

Mo asked, "Are you all right? You look like you've seen a ghost."

A nervous giggle escaped from my lips. "Yeah, kinda."

"My idea for coming to LA upset you *that much*?'

"No."

"So, what is it?"

"Every time I see the East Okeechobee Road exit, I get the same reaction."

"What upsets you about that particular exit?"

"Nana's buried in the Mount Eden Jewish Cemetery off of East Okeechobee Road on Hialeah Drive."

"Do you want to take a detour and see her? We have enough time."

I held up my hands. "No! I can't. I've never been back there since the day of her funeral. The finality of seeing her name and vitals engraved in the stone is too much to bear, so I pretend she is on a cruise." I laughed. "Kinda ironic, isn't it? We just got off a cruise ship, and I'm pretending she's on one."

"Did you look for her on our ship?"

I rolled my eyes. "Of course not. The rational side of me realizes she's dead. But the emotional side can't accept the finality of her death. It's my way of coping." I slid my eyes over to him. "Still want to marry me since you just found out I'm a nut case?"

He laughed. "Absolutely. You're not a nut case. You're merely someone trying to deal with the loss of a loved one."

He cuffed my shoulder. "Holly Lehrman has a nice ring to it, doesn't it?"

"Say it a few times. Let me get a feel for it."

"Holly Lehrman. Holly Lehrman. Holly Lehrman."

I grinned. "I could get used to it. And let's face it, Lehrman is a helluva lot easier to spell and pronounce correctly than Schlivnik."

"So is that a yes?"

"Was that a proposal?'

"It is if you want it to be."

"How about I take it under advisement for the time being?"

He twisted his hand back and forth. "Not as good as a yes, but as the daddios say, it's better than a poke in the nose with a sharp stick."

"Come to LA, at the end of August, and let's see how it goes."

"Done."

We bumped fists to seal the deal.

My stomach jumped a nervous loop-de-loop as we approached the signs for Miami International Airport. Mo turned into the lane marked *departures*, and I squeezed his hand. I fought to keep the tremor out of my voice. "Just drop me off, please, and go."

Mo gave me a hard look. "*That's* the way you want us to part?"

Yes. No. I guess so. Definitely. I think so. Maybe. I dunno. Probably. Yes.

I nodded. "Yes. This is difficult enough without a goodbye scene at the gate."

He blew the air out of his cheeks. "O-kay."

He pulled up to the curb and parked. We got out of the car, and Mo opened the trunk. He hailed a porter, pointed out my bags, and tipped the guy.

Mo pulled me into his arms and held me as if he'd never let me go. His voice cracked as he talked into my hair. "*Te amo. No adiós. Solamente hasta luego*. (I love you. No goodbyes. Only until next time.) Travel safely. Remember to walk using your right foot first as you step onto the plane, the way your Nana told you to. And call me when you land."

I wanted to tell him what was in my heart, but the words were clogged in my throat. Dad's voice spoke inside my head. "*Talk is cheap.*

Actions speak louder than words. Put your money where your mouth is." I cupped Mo's face in my hands and kissed him soundly. It was the best I could do. Was it enough?

His answer was a kiss so deep that it would linger on my lips long after I arrived home. Then, without uttering another word, he got into the convertible and drove away. I stared after it until the car melted into the outbound traffic and disappeared.

Chapter Forty-Five

Between the hustle and bustle of the swimwear market, a murder investigation that almost got me killed, and Mo Lehrman messing up my head and heart, I couldn't get on the plane home fast enough.

The change in cabin air pressure and a strong Bloody Mary combined to knock me for a loop. I was out like a light as we reached cruising level. I settled into a deep slumber, and all of a sudden, a movie started running inside my head.

Mo and I are in the grand ballroom of a cruise ship, dancing at the head of a conga line. In the next scene, we are coming down the gangplank of the cruise ship. Our families and all the other passengers are still on board. They're showering us with confetti and yelling congratulations and mazel tov.

Then the movie switches reels to a different scene. Mo and I are in the back seat of a taxi. The cab drives into a cemetery. I tell the driver which section to stop at. Mo instructs the driver to wait for us, and we get out of the cab. We walk around the graves, and I find a flat granite memorial marker under a palm tree with Nana's vitals etched into the stone. I introduce Mo to Nana. Nana's voice whispers, "Welcome to the family, dahling." Mo and I recite the Kaddish, the prayer for the dead. We say goodbye to Nana, and then we get back into the cab. Mo tells the driver to take us to the departure terminal at Miami International Airport.

Mo turns to me and says, "So, Mrs. Lehrman, what time is our flight home to LA?"

I look at my ring finger. I'm wearing Nana's engagement and wedding rings. Mo is wearing my Grandpa Charlie's ruby and diamond ring on his ring finger. I look at Mo and say, "Baby, say my new name again and again. I'll never get tired of hearing it." Mo grins and says Holly Lehrman over and over and over.

Suddenly, the plane hit turbulence. I was startled awake by the violent jolts and the captain's voice over the intercom, instructing the passengers to take their seats and buckle their seatbelts. I was momentarily confused as to my whereabouts until my ears popped from the altitude change, and I remembered I was on an airplane. I shook my head to clear the cobwebs. What the hell was that wacko dream all about?

And if the dream wasn't weird enough, then the cabin temperature dropped fifty degrees as the gloating ghosts arrived. They performed a victory dance up and down the aisle to celebrate my return to LA. I shooed them away, and miraculously, they disappeared once the turbulence stopped and the flight attendant asked if I cared for another Bloody Mary. Yeah, right. More booze. That's exactly what I need. Not. If a crazy dream like that was the result of one shot of vodka, I'd better stick to a Virgin Mary.

What did the dream mean?

Nana once said, "Dreams are messages your heart sends to your head."

Did my heart message my head to marry Mo?

And if it did, should I listen to it?

If I only knew.

Nana's voice whispered inside my head.

"*Listen to your heart.*

Always trust it.

Your heart will never betray you.

When one door closes, another one opens.

Some things are bershert...just meant to be."

The End.

Don't miss out!

Visit the website below and you can sign up to receive emails whenever Susie Black publishes a new book. There's no charge and no obligation.

https://books2read.com/r/B-A-WWUKF-ZUMFJ

BOOKS 2 READ

Connecting independent readers to independent writers.

About the Author

Named Best US Author of the Year by N. N. Lights Book Heaven, award-winning cozy mystery author Susie Black was born in the Big Apple but now calls sunny Southern California home. Like the protagonist in her Holly Swimsuit Mystery Series, Susie is a successful apparel sales executive. Susie began telling stories as soon as she learned to talk. Now she's telling all the stories from her garment industry experiences in humorous mysteries.

She reads, writes, and speaks Spanish, albeit with an accent that sounds like Mildred from Michigan went on a Mexican vacation and is trying to fit in with the locals. Since life without pizza and ice cream as her core food groups wouldn't be worth living, she's a dedicated walker to keep her girlish figure. A voracious reader, she's also an avid stamp collector and ardent sailor. Susie lives with a highly intelligent man and has one incredibly brainy but smart-aleck adult son who inexplicably blames his sarcasm on an inherited genetic defect.

Looking for more? Contact Susie at:

E-mail: mysteries.authorsusieblack@gmail.com

www.ingramcontent.com/pod-product-compliance
Lightning Source LLC
LaVergne TN
LVHW090604110826
845146LV00001B/254

9798995626114